# Kill Academy

## Kill Series – Book One

RICHARD A. POWELL II

ISBN: 0692884599
ISBN-13: 978-0692884591

# ACKNOWLEDGEMENTS

Thanks to Tracey Shuk, Darrel Messmore, and Amy Powell for taking an early look at the manuscript and giving me feedback. Your help is appreciated more than you know.

To all the people out there that still read books despite the fact there is no book report due tomorrow ... THANK YOU!

www.richardapowellii.com

Other works by Richard A. Powell II:

*RejectGuy99* (2015)
*A Room Full of Keys* (2013)
*Neither Snow, Nor Rain, Nor Zombie Infection & Other Strange Tales* (2012)

Available by order at bookstores and online worldwide

# 1

Sunday

I'm standing in the shadows of an alley, near the corner of the building closest to the street, my black and midnight blue outfit helping me blend into the darkness of the city. I often wear blue tinted sunglasses, even at night, to hide the whites of my eyes, an often-overlooked technique in urban warfare. My short stature and slim physique help too. I'm definitely not supermodel thin, as I just love pizza too much, but I'm crazy flexible and can run and run and run. All these attributes go a long way in keeping me alive in this Hell of a place.

I grew up on these streets – mean streets, primal. Normal people don't come to this part of town, where the rejects, the snakes, the unwelcome make their way. It wouldn't take much for a Privi, that's what we call a Privileged Individual, to take a wrong turn down here, knock on the wrong door, and POOF! They'd never be seen or heard from again, lost to these soulless animals.

Not all of us are evil bastards. Some of us, and I include myself in that lot, have simply been dealt a bad hand in the game of life and can see no other way to exist, and there never seems an easy way to escape. Eventually, no matter how hard us Good Ones try to rise above the clutch of these streets, we get absorbed into the mess - a dead end road driven down long ago with no room left in our hearts or minds for remembering how to turn around.

It's about 11 pm, not much traffic on the street, Sunday. A couple of guys are hanging out in front of the liquor store across the way, the one on the left smoking a cigarette like he's the coolest asshole on the block. I rolled my eyes the second I saw him. The other guy just keeps looking up and down the street, his lips pursed like he's always in deep thought or trying to impress a girl, not sure which. His head slowly bobs to some unknown song – the soundtrack of his life, I guess. I want nothing more than to sneak up next to them and hit their Achilles tendons with a blade. But I won't. Again, NOT evil, but I'd probably be doing society a solid on that one. Whatever. I have something I actually need to do, the real reason I'm lurking in the dark.

In the criminal underground, one thing a person should not do is have a schedule and repeat stupid criminal behavior on that schedule so that you can easily be tracked. I swear, I want to tear my hair out at the general incompetence of the average thug. Fucking nitwits is what they are. If one is choosing to engage in the Illegal Arts, the main goal should always be: Don't ... Get ... Caught. This rule, however, is always disregarded as somehow unnecessary with a mockingly stupid hubris that belongs on the middle school playground and not here, a place where people die, easily, every day. If there was a code of conduct down here, it was tossed out with the old-school gangsters long ago.

From what I can see, the only oddity on the block tonight at this particular time is myself and a pristine, late model, navy blue town car parked about four spots down to my left. I can see someone sitting in the driver's seat. Not sure what they're doing but I need to keep an eye on them. I don't like surprises. I've done my research, and they don't fit.

Why do I mention all this about schedules and normality? Well, tonight, like every Sunday at about 11:10 pm, a black SUV of miscreants from the Battle Boys gang will pull into the alley, do a little business with Freddy Vegas - not his real name. He's an overly stereotypical Italian with slicked back black hair, a Mario Brothers mustache, and a black member's only jacket. He must be the last member, the one who didn't get the memo that they closed the club in 1988.

Tonight, they exchange the backpack of crank, several hundred teeny-tiny zippy bags of it, for a brown paper bag with ten grand in cash. Then my work begins.

I casually scoot back to my car, parked a building down, and follow them for a short time until I'm sure they are on their way to their next highly predictable location. I screech around the next corner, a right on Madison Way, and take a preplanned shortcut at high speed to get ahead of them on their path, a full three miles ahead.

Like a good little damsel-in-distress, I wait on the side of the road with the hood of my aging, black Chevy Caprice wide open, my hazards on, the positive side terminal plug pulled off the battery so the car won't start, and my forced womanly nature on full display hiding the underlying guile. In the honest part of my life, the feminist in me would never allow the use of my sexuality to get what I want. I despise the idea of it, however, when it comes to dipshits like the Battle Boys, I will wear my acting chops proudly.

I had removed my sunglasses and the jacket, which revealed blue eye shadow and a two sizes too small pink scoop neck t-shirt, and beneath that a white tank and an uncomfortable but effective pushup bra of white lace. I don't have an abundance to work with in the chest department so I do what I have to do, true commitment to my craft. I don't think I own another bra besides that one. And, to top it off, if I put my hands in the air, my midriff will miraculously expose itself. Something I have on deck, just in case.

No sooner have I positioned myself near the front of the car, ready to lean in for an absent-minded look at my engine, the headlights of a certain SUV shine bright from just up the road. Good. I'm tired and ready to go home. The preparations for my little heist have left me ready for a few days out to sea on my yacht – The S.S. Mine Now. I had changed the name from The S.S. Minnow. How fucking original on that asshole's part, right? I went out the first night and used a razor blade to scratch off the old name, and with a purple permanent marker wrote the new name with big fat letters, graffiti style. Besides, after what he did, taking his boat was the least of what I really should have done to him. But that, I'll get to later.

As the SUV gets closer, I come around to the driver's side of my car and place both hands on the edge. To really sell it, I bend over slightly and hike up my ass, peering into the engine compartment with a side eye on the incoming package. Won't it be something if they don't even stop? Let's be real though. They'll stop. A vehicle full of twenty-something, overwrought, criminal Neanderthals with an over-inflated sense of power and worth passing up an opportunity to force themselves on some unsuspecting woman, one in need of assistance on a lonely road just outside of town? Yeah, right.

Like I thought they would, as they approach, they slow down to assess the situation. Once they see me leaning over all helpless and vulnerable, desperate for a big, strong man to rescue me, they pull in right behind my car.

Before pulling my upper body out from under the hood, I tilt my head slowly from left to right to stretch out my neck muscles, and roll my shoulders back three times to do the same. I have to stay limber if I intend to successfully take on all four of the men in that SUV, and I use the word 'men' here loosely. Shouldn't be a problem. Won't be the first time, nor the last. It's so funny how in these situations they always dramatically underestimate the ability and power of a tiny woman who's pissed off. Always works to my advantage with the guppies.

Three of them exit the black Suburban, making their way toward me. I'm worried about what the fourth one is doing, probably just staying with the SUV to guard the cash and any other product that might be in there, but I ponder the possibilities nonetheless.

"Oh poop. I just don't know what happened," I say with

all the vulnerable airhead I can muster. "Thank you so much for stopping. You guys know anything about cars?"

The leader of the three quickly steps around to my left, brushing his hand along the waistline of my back. It takes every ounce of patience I hold to not snap his hand right from his wrist, but I'm not ready to engage, so I gulp and keep up appearances.

The other two stand back a few feet but are clearly ready to pounce if given the instruction to do so. One of them keeps popping the knuckles on his hands, the smaller one pays little attention to what is happening, instead choosing to play on his phone and only glancing up every ten seconds or so.

"Well, babe, let's just take a look and see what we got here," the leader says, towering over me at probably a little over six feet tall. He makes no effort to check the car, looking me up and down instead. He tries hard to hide the half rotten teeth in his mouth as he speaks, no doubt from dipping into the meth they regularly sell. He smells of weed and stale beer and un-deodorized armpit. Disgusting creature.

I grow more and more concerned about the wildcard still in the SUV, so I decide to see if I can push things along, and maybe toward their vehicle. No doubt they're all carrying firearms, so however I end up handling the situation, it must be fierce and fast.

"Hey, I got an idea," I pronounce with fake enthusiasm. "Any chance you fellas could give me a quick ride? Not far from here, I swear. My name's Holly by the way." Even as I say the words, I can't believe these mongoloids are falling for my act. I hadn't put any thought into my name either, should they have asked, so I used the first ditzy one that came to mind.

"I'm Banger," the leader says with two fist bumps to his own chest. "That retard with the phone is Myles, and that buff sumbitch is Rico Sauvé. So, you wants a ride, huh?" Banger looks over to the other two. "You guys think we can give her," he stops and makes a pelvic grinding motion that he thinks I don't see, "a ride?"

Knuckle cracking meathead Rico Sauvé chimes in. "Oh yeah. We can definitely do that." He nods and licks his lips.

My third eye rolls all the way back into head. I can't help but fantasize about how much I am going to enjoy whooping their asses.

"Yeah, whatever you guys wanna do," Myles finally says having no idea what the hell is going on. He immediately goes back to his phone.

I know right then he is going to be the easiest one to deal with, so he will be last. Hard targets first, soft ones last, at least in my book.

"Come here, honey," Banger asks of me as he walks back to their SUV. He motions with his right hand. "Come on. We gotta ask Marco if we can give you a ride."

Reluctantly, I do a little hot trot with bent wrists to the rear driver's side of the SUV.

Banger knocks twice on the tinted window. Three seconds later, it rolls down and from the darkness, the side of a bearded face emerges. I can't make out any other features.

"Hey, Marco, ummm, hang on a second," he says before putting up his index finger. He looks at me. "What's your name again, honey?"

"Holly," I answer with bubbles and sparkles floating through my words. Clearly, he had been too busy checking out my assets to hear my name.

Banger turns back to the open window. "Holly here is broken down and wants to know if we can give her ride?" He raises his eyebrows twice, quickly.

Ten seconds pass. Finally, a hand emerges from the dark calling Banger closer. He obliges. Whispers ensue. He steps back and turns to me. The door opens.

"Go ahead and slide in there, baby. We'll join you in a minute."

I don't like the tone. I think about it for a second and quickly realize the guy in the car is most likely hard target number one and will need to be taken out first, so being alone with him might be the perfect opportunity to split these guys up.

I step up to the SUV and gingerly slide into the backseat, shutting the door behind me. Banger walks back to my car to join his buddies in wait.

For about three minutes, the SUV rocks and shakes like someone is having a grand ol' time. During the ruckus, I can hear the boys outside give an occasional WHOOP WHOOP or GO GET IT BOSS. They wait patiently but are all eager to get a crack at me. They do take the opportunity to search my car, everywhere but my trunk, of course, which is locked and I have the keys on me. There is nothing for them to find though in the rest of the vehicle as I never leave any identifying information in the car in case it has to be dumped in a hurry, something I do every three or four months anyway. I find it easier to keep a low profile by replacing my piece of shit car with another piece of shit car every few months - anything that runs for under a thousand dollars from Bill Wesson's Auto Ranch. They take cash, don't ask fucking questions, and pretend like they have never seen me before each and every time I come around for another POS. I assume they think I am running from an abusive ex-boyfriend. Then again, in the part of town they operate in, they are likely much more aware of the seedy nature of their average customer and simply choose to be oblivious. Good for business and good for me.

When the moving and shaking cease, I quietly open the opposite car door to the one I entered in, and crawl over the now unconscious Marco. When I entered, I introduced myself and asked his name. He replied and I leaned in. Before that asshole could even think about putting a hand on me, I gave him a chop to the throat, limiting his airflow and crushing his voice box. I pulled off the pink t-shirt I was wearing, leaving only the white tank and pushup bra, and used it to tie Marco's hands behind his back. I peeked over his shoulder and saw the brown paper bag. After I grabbed it and placed it by the door to my left, I straddled Marco and looked deep into his rage filled eyes as he struggled to breath.

"Glad to have met you, dipshit," I said just before swinging my right elbow into the side of his head, knocking him clean out. The bone on bone contact actually sent a mild stinger up my arm, but it disappeared after a few seconds. It was then I took a minute to shake and bounce the SUV to mimic a little sexy-time action before exiting on the passenger side.

I wait near the front of the vehicle, ducking down as not to be seen until ready to strike. I can hear the guys discussing whether they should check to see if Marco is done. If they open that car door, the charade is over and guns might start blazing. I leave the bag of money on the ground near the front tire and sneak around to behind the SUV.

"Let me see what's up," Banger says, getting closer to me with each word.

I take in and release three quick breaths to focus myself, and as Banger puts his hand on the door handle, I emerge at his right side with a big, fake smile on my face, all my teeth showing.

He jumps back a little and turns to face me, a look of utter confusion on his ugly face. "What the fu."

I don't let him get the word out from behind his rotten teeth, interrupting him with a swift right uppercut to the chin. A few teeth and blood project from his mouth in time with his head flying backward. He is so completely unprepared for it, his feet actually leave the ground and he falls back and onto the ground with a thud, out cold. Guess I overestimated his target level. Not that I expected much.

Moving fast, I run to the next closest one, Rico. I counted on this muscle-bound freak to be little harder to take down, so I came prepared. While on the move, I reach into my left, lower leg cargo pants pocket and produce my stun gun.

He appears much more prepared for me than Banger, his scowl and clutched fists, an example. He shows no worry about taking down little ol' me.

But little ol' me has a big, bad equalizer. When I get to

within about three feet of him, I thrust my left hand up as I turn the safety off and press the trigger. The two probes fly out and pierce Rico in the area between his upper abs and his man breasts. He jolts a bit, staying on his feet, and rather than being incapacitated like I had hoped, he is kind of pissed.

He yanks the probes from his chest, tossing them down furiously. Before I can even react, he uses both his hands to grab me by my arms, just below the shoulders. With no effort, he lifts my body off the ground, digging his fingers in, and tosses me across the hood of the SUV. The stun gun falls to the ground at his feet.

I slide head first right over the edge and onto the ground just past the bag of money I had left. I land on my bad right shoulder, a recurring painful injury from three years ago when I suffered nerve damage after being stabbed just below my collar bone. My face hits hard on the gravel too. I said it before – mean streets.

I do a silent scream, not wanting to give Rico the impression he can hurt me. I know I don't have time to play around, so I brush off the pain, get to me feet but stay low enough to not be seen, and grab the money. When Rico emerges at the front of the SUV, I unsheathe the four-inch blade from my right ankle and plunge it into the side of his left knee. I twist the knife a quarter turn before pulling it out. A steady stream of blood pours from the wound turning his faded jeans red. Our feet shuffle. We've managed to exchange places.

"Ah!" he screams as he buckles.

I wind up and kick him square in his face, forcing him back and into the roadside ditch about five feet from the edge of the road.

With no time to waste, I throw eyes at Myles. He's standing near the rear of my car, on the driver's side, a small black gun drawn and pointed at me, both his hands on it and shaking.

"Don't move, you, you, stupid bitch."

"Myles, honey, these guys attacked me." I play contrite and

innocent. "They hurt me." I reveal to him the bloody scuff on the side of my face from when I hit the ground. I inch closer, taking a tiny step with every few words. "You're not like them, Myles," I say, shaking my head. "I can tell. You're nice. You're not like them."

"I told you not to move. Now stop," he trembles.

I see the toil in his eyes. I feign a few tears and a quivering lip. "Please don't shoot me." I take another step. "I just wanna go home." Another step. I am five feet from him and blocking the left headlight of the SUV. A chill takes to the air, and with just my push-up bra and tank on up top, goose pimples cover my arms. I place the paper bag out in front of me.

"Why do you have that? Who the hell are you?" he asks, beginning to doubt my act.

"Just take it and let me go home, I just wanna go home." Time is running short. At any moment, one or more of the other three men might wake up and I'll be in deep shit. "Please, Myles. Please."

He shakes his head, a firm answer to my plea.

"I'm just going to sit this down here," I say, leaning to my left as I slowly move the bag down to the ground. Out of the corner of my eye, I witness my opportunity.

For the briefest of moments, Myles relaxes his grip on the gun, following the bag with the barrel instead of keeping it on me.

I let go of the bag and send my right leg flying through the air with a firm kick to his hands, forcing him to release gun. It tumbles away, skidding into the street before landing in the dirt across the road, lost in the brush and dark of night.

Myles panics a bit and runs after the gun but soon realizes it's a lost cause. Standing in the middle of the street, he stops and turns back to me.

I snatch the money from the ground and look him square in the face. "You're not going to hurt me, Myles. You're not going to hurt a girl, but let me assure you, if you don't let me get in my car and get the hell outta here, I'm sure enough going to kick the living shit out of you."

He gulps and remains still, silent.

"Now be a good little boy and go back to your car, but you might want to help Rico first. He's bleeding out right now. His left knee. Wrap it up real tight with a t-shirt or a towel or something to try and stop the bleeding."

I chance it and just walk away. I throw the bag in the front seat of my car, leaving the door open, and reattach the terminal to the battery before slamming the hood shut. I'm surprised to find Myles still catatonic in the middle of the road.

"Hey! Go help Rico or he's a dead man. Go right now!"

He obeys.

I hustle my ass into the car and off I go. Confident he won't follow, I don't bother to look back.

Back at my yacht, I pour myself a brandy with four ice cubes and drink the entire glass before pouring a second. I leave the glass on my bedside table. I strip off all my clothes, go to the bathroom, and put the shower on full hot. I find a bottle of naproxen sodium, fast-acting gel caps, and down two with a splash of water from the sink. The real me inspects reverse mirror me and the scratch on the side of her face.

"Thanks, Rico, you son of a bitch. Of course, I did take your boss' money and stab you in the knee, but hey, let's not play the blame game. You're an unscrupulous bastard, and though I may not be sugar and spice and all things nice, my intentions are fuckin' elevated."

I rotate my sore arm and can't get a full revolution without excruciating pain. I wince and stop after two attempts. I hope the meds and the booze will help. With a sufficient steaming of the bathroom, I step into the stall and enjoy a long, hot shower.

As my mind whirls with the events of the evening, I can't help but think of the Leer kids. It's been a while since my last visit and I know they will be needing some of the money I relieved my Battle Boy friends of. I have grown to love the Leer family, perhaps the closest thing I have ever had to one of my own, but it's terribly difficult to face them sometimes knowing what I know about their father's death. Nineteen-year-old Gabby is now raising her four younger siblings basically off their dad's social security and Gabby's job at a department store. I assist whenever I can and they've never really understood why. Not sure I ever want them to know.

# 2

Monday

I wake up later than expected and the stiffness has set in. I creak and hobble out of bed, take a piss, down two more pain pills, and blink my way through a few drops of eye moisturizing fluid. I think the ocean air from living on the docks gives me itchy, dry eyes, something that never happened to me before my yacht days.

I stare into the mirror and think about giving myself a little self-talk about bad choices, where I'm headed, what I hope to accomplish, but instead I say fuck it and just run wet fingers through my mess of a haircut – which is really just simple shoulder length with no bangs, a flatter version of Jennifer Aniston from *Friends*, except dark brunette. I'll end up throwing my hoodie over it most of the day anyway. As long as I don't look anything like I did last night. I don't want any Battle Boys recognizing me. Which reminds me – probably time to get another car, just in case. It'll be a month earlier than usual but a girl's got to do what a girl's got to do.

I kick around the mess of clothes scattered about the floor and find a pair of khaki cargo pants with some change still in one of the pockets and a red hoodie that doesn't smell too foul. After dressing, I drop my cell phone in one pants pocket and my keys on the other side, transfer six grand of the money from the original bag into another paper bag and a few crisp hundred dollar bills into my own wallet, and shove that into my right back pocket. Yes, I carry a man's wallet and not a purse. I've always found it easier. A purse is just so ... girlie, and a fanny pack is out of the fucking question.

With a bottled iced tea from the fridge, off I go on the three-block walk from the yacht to where I had parked the car. I always do it that way. Another line of defense. Anyone who has ever seen me at the docks would not have seen how I got there, short of walking up from Harris Street.

As I approach the car, I have the distinct impression eyes are on me. Surreptitiously, I pull a coin from my pocket and drop it on the ground, giving me an excuse to bend over and turn. With only my eyes, I quickly survey the sidewalks and the street. Traffic is light, pedestrians minimal.

There's a guy reading a newspaper at the bus stop bench but he's always there this time of day. Plus, how cliché would that disguise be. Two middle-aged women walk together on the other side of the street, chatting away, oblivious to their surroundings. Nothing odd there. A few seconds later, those women pass a building where a sharp-dressed, tall, black man stands against the brick façade. His sunglasses hide his gaze. He fiercely smokes a cigarette like a man on a break from work. Problem is, what business on this block full of old warehouses, a secondhand furniture store, and a community outreach center would have an employee dressed like a Park Avenue attorney? Not to mention, there is a familiarity to him I can't place.

I decide to take a detour rather than go straight to my car. I figure that after five or ten minutes he'll be gone, and if not, well ... he'll be dealt with.

I place the coin back in my pocket and walk right past my car without a glance. I make a left on Lawrence and stop in an old bookstore I've been to before. Some classic rock plays on a radio while the clerk thumbs on his cell phone. He lifts his head to acknowledge me but doesn't say anything. I flip through a few stacks in the science fiction section before disappearing back out the door without the clerk noticing. I would have sensed the air pressure in the room change when the door opened, but hey, that's just me.

Upon returning to the block where my car is, everything seems normal - no oddities, decent after school traffic, and most importantly, no smoking stranger. I hop in my car and head to the Leer house.

The northeast side of town has seen better days. Most of the houses have paint peeling, shingles missing, weeds replacing most of the grass, cracked sidewalks, but mostly good people from the school of hard knocks. Where the south-end is the de facto criminal, lowlife hangout, the place where all money came through drug deals and extortion and theft (wink, wink), the northeast side houses the working poor, some college housing, the barely escaped south-siders, and the Leer family.

I park right in front of the 1930s, white, two-story house. Moss spatters the siding where the water drips from breached gutters. I grab the rusting wrought iron handrail as I walk up the hard right-leaning concrete stairs that lead up to the covered porch.

Butterflies churn in my stomach each and every time I arrive at this door but I know I have to do it. Nothing that happened in the past is the fault of these kids. Nothing. I owe them more than I will ever be able to give them. The six grand I brought will help, but some sins, some actions, there is no reconciliation for.

I close my eyes and take in a few deep breaths. I press the doorbell with my right thumb and take one step back. I lean back a bit and glance over both shoulders, eyes and ears on everything. I have a built-in, high-functioning, sonar-like sense of my surroundings. Occupational hazard. It took only a few times getting snuck up on and getting my ass whooped before that tool developed and it has served me well.

The front door flies open and sixteen-year-old Pete Leer appears. He barely makes eye contact, his mind on other things.

"Come in," he says as he walks away, back to the dining room table to engage the laptop sitting there. He has grown since my last visit, easily a few inches taller than me now.

I step in a few feet, shut the door behind me, and wait.

"Is Gabby home yet?" She is the eldest of the Leer children at nineteen but still very much a child in my book, though life and taking care of her siblings in the absence of their parents has forced her coming of age much faster than she deserves. She is actually quite brilliant and street smart. I would like to see her go to college and make something out of herself, but I understand the logistical nightmare that would be. If I could afford them a nanny, I wouldn't hesitate. The bag of money I brought will help for a few months, but it will only keep them from sinking, it will not take them out of the quicksand.

Pete points toward the back of the house to where the kitchen is. His eyes never leave the screen.

I walk past the long, banquet style table and just as I hit the archway leading to the kitchen, I'm damn near knocked off my feet with a charging hug from nine-year-old Evie.

"Josey!" She squeezes me so tight I almost can't breathe.

I lightly hug her back. "Alright, kiddo. Good to see you too."

She lets go her grip and looks up to me, eyes wide and smiling. "I got straight A's again on my report card."

I make eye contact briefly with Gabby as she stirs a pot of boiling pasta on the stovetop. I bring my attention back to the little brown-haired, blue-eyed Evie. "Of course you did, silly. You're brilliant." I rub the top of her head and walk over to the peninsula, taking a seat on the end bar stool facing Gabby.

"Evie, will you please run upstairs and tell the twins that dinner is in ten minutes?" Gabby asks after checking inside the oven at the garlic bread. My mouth waters from the waft of butter and garlic.

The youngest of the Leers sprints away and up the stairs. She's wearing a sky-blue pair of Converse All-Stars. I don't know that I've ever seen her without them on. When her feet outgrow them, she insists on buying the same ones, same color, only larger.

I place the paper bag on the counter, not to draw attention to it, but just to get it out of my hand.

"Been a while. I was beginning to think you moved away or something," Gabby says.

"Yeah, just ... busy ya know. How's the world of big box retail treating ya?"

Gabby grabs a pot holder from the counter and uses it to remove the bread from the oven, placing it on the stovetop next to the two pots - one of boiling pasta, the other of a simmering red sauce. While continuing our conversation, she drains the noodles, returns them to the pan, pours the sauce over them, and stirs.

"Good. Finally got promoted to assistant manager. More money but longer hours. Have to work six days a week often."

"I don't know how you do it. I couldn't keep a goldfish alive let alone four siblings. And they're all okay, school and everything?"

"Pretty good, mostly. Randy has not taken well to his pre-algebra, but Mandy is helping him through it. They may be twins but they sure have their differences."

"Well, they are fraternal twins. You can't even tell they're related by looking at them, at least not past the blonde hair and blue eyes."

"True. Oh, Pete just got his license. He's trying to find a job after school so he can buy a car. We'll probably never see him again once that happens."

I chuckle. "He's a smart kid. He'll find his way outta here and you should encourage him."

Gabby thinks for a moment about the truth behind that and ultimately agrees.

Evie returns from upstairs and pounces into the stool next to me, elbows on the counter, face in her hands, her fluttering eyes and shit-eating grin lock on me. I ignore her for the moment.

"Evie, dear, would you please grab the salad bowl from the fridge and put in on the table. And tell Pete to clear his crap out of there, it's time to eat."

"Josey?" Evie asks with a tone that suggests I might not like the question.

"Yes."

"What happened to your face?"

"Evie, don't bother her and please do as I asked," Gabby blurts.

"I will, geez. I'm just curious. I have an inquisitive mind."

"Can you even spell inquisitive?" Gabby jokes.

"Awfully big vocabulary for a girl your age," I say.

"I'm almost ten. I watch the Science Channel and the History Channel now."

Incredulous, I ask, "Do they even have shows about history on the History Channel anymore?"

Evie hops off her stool and does as she was instructed by her big sister. "Well, no. But they have tons of shows on Bigfoot, and I find that hairy beast fascinating." She leaves the room with the salad bowl and two bottles of dressing in hand.

"Kids? When did they learn to talk like that?" Gabby places a large spoon in the pot of bowtie pasta and sauce.

"I don't know, but it's kind of unnerving. I'm only twenty-three and they make me feel like such an idiot."

Gabby nods. "You're welcome to eat with us."

"No. I just," I pick up the paper bag to make her aware of it, "brought you a little something. You know I promised your dad I would look out for you, and I know I haven't been around in a bit." Gabby knows exactly what is in the bag. I use the same technique every time.

"You don't have to do that anymore. We're doing fine. Really."

I open my mouth to speak but feet pounding on the steps interrupts the words about to escape my lips. Mandy and Randy, the twelve-year-old twins, chase after one another, stopping briefly to wave at me before continuing their game of tag.

Gabby shouts, "Can you two knuckleheads come in here and grab the pasta and bread and take it to the table?" They respond immediately, Randy taking the pasta, Mandy the bread. Gabby removes five plates and five bowls from the cupboard and sits them on the counter in front of me. "It's like a zoo in here sometimes. You looked like you were going to say something."

"Yeah, I know you guys are doing fine. You really should get a fuckin' award for how well you handle things around here."

Gabby smiles. "Probably."

"It's important to me. I made a promise."

"Not sure I want to know, but I still don't understand where all the money comes from."

"I told you. It's better tax wise if I give it to you in cash."

"You didn't rob a bank, did you?"

"No." I'm not lying.

"This isn't from some drug deal you made?"

My eyes almost go wide. "No." I clear my throat. "Nothing like that." That is mostly true. Somebody made a drug deal. I just did a little payment interruptus. I'm not sure she believes me.

"I don't want your money if it's dirty."

"I can understand that." That is the best diversion response I can muster without really addressing her concern. "I really need to run, got things to do. Go eat your dinner and keep keeping on. I'll stop by again soon when I can visit longer. Is that ok?"

"Definitely. Evie sure loves you."

I try not to read too deep into the comment but it's hard.

I smile. "I love her too." I stand up and motion for her to walk before me. I follow her to the table.

I stand for a moment and marvel at the Leer family. I've always imagined life with a big family, away from the children's home and bad foster situations. It nearly brings a tear to my eye. I want to be a part of them but I won't allow myself to get too close. I just can't. I would feel like a liar and an imposter.

Evie runs over to me and hugs me again, even harder this time. She is more perceptive than I realize.

"I want you to stay," Evie says as she releases me.

"I'll be back soon, I promise, and we'll play Uno or something, and I'll bring that pizza you like."

"Come Saturday," Evie demands.

"Not that soon, but soon. It was good to see you all again but I gotta scoot. Enjoy your dinner and be good for your big sis."

There is a smattering of responses from all the kids with mouthfuls of food. Gabby is still standing, not wanting to be rude. I take the hint and walk toward the front door.

Gabby follows, then steps around me. She opens the door and I start to walk through.

"Josey?"

"Yeah."

She just looks at me with a sad sort of smile. She mouths the words 'thank you' and lets out a sigh.

I nod, wave, quickly turn around, and leave. I don't look back until I get into my car. I rub my face with both hands and hold back tears. Like every time I have visited them, I held an urge to reveal the truth about Wayne, their father, and what really happened the night he was killed. They are owed the truth. It would not be easy to hear, nor would it be easy for me to say, but some part of me is compelled nonetheless to do so. They would likely never speak to me again, and I could never blame them for that. It's just becoming so hard to live the lie.

# 3

Headquarters of the Organization – Boss' Office

Madame K sits in the leather chair behind her desk, left leg crossing over the right, her elbows on the armrests, and her hands together with just the fingertips touching. Her open laptop reveals a series of photos taken over the course of a few weeks. Folder labeled: J Baldwin.

Standing behind the two chairs opposite her desk are Tolliver Washington - second in command of the organization, and Dina Whiteside - the acting recruit evaluator and team therapist.

"I think you might be losing your touch, Tolliver," Madam K says, matter of fact. She refuses at that point to make any eye contact with either of her subordinates, instead staring right past them.

Ollie doesn't reply. He knows how pissed off she really is. Everyone calls him Ollie and she only ever calls him Tolliver when she is angry. He doesn't reply.

"She saw you, multiple times. Covert mean anything to you people anymore?" Madame K says.

Ollie opens his mouth to speak but a quick raised hand by his boss forces him to choke back his words.

"Rhetorical," Madame K says. She put her hand down and onto her knee. "Her skillset is clearly spot on. The question

23

is," she pauses to collect her thoughts, "Will she do what we need her to do, what she'll be paid to do?" Madame K throws her eyes to Dina.

"She's done it before, at least once that we know of," Dina responds.

"Yeah, but it still bothers her a great deal," Ollie adds. "She visits that family too, gives them money. What does that tell you?"

Madame K is still, pondering the words of her two most trusted advisors.

"I believe she can be shown the benefit of our services, the altruistic nature of it," Dina says. "She has a real Robin Hood thing going, which is a side of her we can appeal to. It will take some work, no doubt, but I'm confident we can get her there."

"Abilities wise, there is no question. I mean, Jesus, we all saw the photos of those four guys from last night. She can handle herself," Ollie says.

"She sure handled you," Madame K interrupts.

Ollie smirks before continuing. "Exactly, but my concern is the ethical problem, scruples versus turpitude. I don't see the killer in her. Maybe in defense of someone, to save someone, sure, but preemptive, non-suspect targeting, I have doubts."

"Orphaned, grew up on the streets of the south end, took out four Battle Boys without even using a gun." Dina put her hands in the air. "I haven't seen a more qualified candidate since Amatto."

"Amatto was an angry young man and hated everyone, hated the world, still does" Ollie says. "I'm not questioning whether she CAN do the job, I'm questioning if she WILL. We never worried whether Amatto would, and now here he is being elevated to Lone Status a full two years earlier than usual."

"We need to make a decision now if she is going to be included in this class of recruits." Madame K rises from her chair and looks to Dina. "What is your vote, Dina?"

"One hundred percent yes."

"Ollie?"

"I have one last concern."

"Do tell," Madame K responds.

"What about her parents?"

"What about them?"

"Well, if she ever got wind of the truth, it might be an issue."

Madame K ponders the idea. It wasn't the first time she has considered the possible ramifications of the truth getting back to Josey. *The organization always comes before any personal concerns,* she thinks. *However, we must assess all risk. She is possibly the most talented recruit we've had in years. That might be all the more reason to be cautious.*

"Your concern is duly noted. I have deeply contemplated that very issue. All things on the table, I am willing to take a chance. She has shown beyond a doubt her abilities, her keen awareness, a sagacity beyond her years, and a strong sensibility toward fighting for the greater good. I say we put her to the test."

"Okay. I guess my vote is yes, though it sounds like I would have been outnumbered two-to-one anyway," Ollie says.

"With Josey, the only way we're going to figure out the answer is to train her and put her in the trenches," Dina says.

"Good, it's decided then. Approach her tomorrow. Now bugger off you two. I have a few calls to make." Madame K sits back down and immediately pulls a cell phone from the right-hand upper drawer of her desk. Her mind quickly turns to other matters while Ollie and Dina leave the office.

# 4

Monday Evening

With the constant worry of being followed on my mind, I decide to head over to my favorite car dealer and do the ol' swap-a-roo. I arrive at the lot an hour before they close. There are no other customers that I can see and not nearly as many cars to choose from as I would normally prefer. Hank, my usual sales guy comes out of the little three room building that reminds me more of an oversized shed than a respectable place of business.

"Hank."

"Back so soon?"

I wobble my head. "Life is ... complicated. Need to trade that POS in and get a fresh one."

"I heard that. The usual?"

"Oh yeah. I got twenty-five hundred but don't really want to spend it all."

"I just got a navy-blue Oldsmobile in. Damn near a hundred fifty thousand miles but still purring like a kitten."

"It doesn't have to purr, it just has to run."

"I promise you it will do that."

"How much?"

"Well, ya know, seeing as how you're pretty much my number one customer." Hank rubs his moustache and does the math in his head. "I'd say fifteen hundred'll get you off the lot."

I say nothing, just stare into his eyes, no emotion on my face. Right when he is starting to get worried and about to speak, I spare him.

"Fifteen is great. Thanks again. Swap the plates, you know the drill."

"Same PO box on the paperwork as before?"

I nod.

"I'll be right back with the keys and the paperwork for you to sign. Sit pretty." He starts to walk away then stops suddenly and turns back around. "We're about to close soon. You want a get a drink or something after we're done?"

"Don't make it weird ... Hank." I put a little sauce on his name when I say it. "But thank you anyway."

Hank points down the row to my right. "Car's down on the end there. Go take a looksee and I'll meet you down there. Just take a sec."

I wave and nod. I glance around the lot. Nothing churning. The street has very little traffic. It's only been a day and I still haven't heard anything about my collection of the dickhead tax from the Battle Boys. I guarantee they are on the lookout for the more delicate me and my soon to be former vehicle. I sign all official documents as Joe Baldwin, not a far stretch from my actual name as I sometimes go by Jo, so if anyone ever comes sniffing around, Hank can show them the paperwork and tell them a guy sold it to him. The PO Box is one of five different ones I keep that I only check two to three times a year, so very difficult to track me down there.

I get to the Olds and am actually impressed by the condition. Must have been some granny's ride, but it's older than I expected too. Has to be considering the number of miles. Either that or grandma had a hell of a commute to bingo.

I open the driver's side front door and briefly poke my head in for look. Super clean. Fabric is gray and worn but no worse than most of the cars I get. Lots of space.

I have never fallen in love with a car as they are purely utilitarian for me, though I am human and I do fantasize of mid-sized SUVs with leather, heated seats, a smooth and quiet ride, and no odd smell that never goes away. I can't see a path that will ever lead me to a normal life, whatever the hell that is, but I'd settle for a night with happy dreams of an ordinary life, one without having to look over my shoulder, without the faces of ugly men doing ugly things, without my hands covered in blood. Even one night might change me forever.

I drive off the lot exhausted, emotionally and physically. I know exactly what I need to feel good, and if I hurry, Jane, the lady who runs the animal shelter on the edge of town will still be there finishing up for the day and I can help her out for an hour. My erratic lifestyle would simply never allow me to have a pet, so I volunteer once and a while, mostly for selfish reasons, I admit, but I dare anyone to surround themselves with doggies and kitties for a bit and deny the dramatically improved mood. Works for me.

# 5

Tuesday

I hit a coma-like sleep about an hour after getting home from the animal shelter. I often need a bit of a winding down period after a 'job', but this last one took more than usual from my energy banks. Getting thrown across the hood of a car and landing on your bad shoulder in a gravel filled ditch will do that. By the time I wake up, around 10 am, my shoulder is better than expected and the scuff on my face is halfway to normal.

I rush off the yacht and down to my new ride, which takes a few extra minutes to find as I'm still unconsciously hunting around for the old car. I even panic for second before I realize my error.

I stop by a private mailbox business, one of many I rotate between, to pick up an envelope before heading to my actual intended destination.

I had set up an appointment to have a coffee with Janelle Pescaglia, just so we could catch up and make sure she wasn't being bothered by one James Orwell. I sometimes regret not just wasting that asshole, but I felt relatively confident he wouldn't be a bother. Plus, I got a place to live out of the deal. One can never be one hundred percent sure, however, so I will keep an eye on Janelle, at least for a few months.

I found her bound and gagged a little over a month ago on the yacht I now call home, a yacht once owned by Mr. Orwell. Well, technically, he still owns it, but he is forbidden from using it. When I am done with it, I'll probably set it on fire.

How I came to follow him back to that boat was sheer happenstance, and as it turns out, fortuitous for me and Janelle both.

Ten weeks ago, I was strolling through The Boardwalk, a local ocean side amusement and shopping area that I frequent to clear my head and play a game of skeeball, maybe win a prize or two for Evie. Ok, I admit, I once kept a stuffed, white tiger but let's not focus on that.

As I sat on a bench picking at a funnel cake and watching the people weave in and out of various areas, I spotted a guy in a red short-sleeved polo shirt and khaki pants just standing near the entrance to the bathrooms, laying eyes on all the females as they walked by, but especially when they entered and exited the bathroom. His outfit came off funny to me, like a guy who didn't know how to dress casual and trying too hard to fit in. He failed. As creepy guys go, his raging seventies moustache was what really should have set off the alarms but it didn't for some reason. It was when I got a clear look at his face, however, that his soul revealed itself to me. His eyes spoke of something sinister, plotting, and devious.

The tracker and planner in me took note and watched for fifteen minutes. He took special interest in one young woman as she entered the restroom, looking her up and down more than once as she walked in his direction. The expression on his face changed as she glanced over at him with a friendly smile before pushing the bathroom door open. Only a man wrapped up in a fantasy world where he was special and desired could take an innocent, empty gesture from a passing woman and convolute the meaning to fit his own corrupt narrative. And that is exactly what he did.

He waited patiently, stroking that ridiculous moustache,

the fingers on his other hand dancing on his upper thigh in high anticipation. He followed the woman and her two friends off The Boardwalk and to the car they arrived in together. He wrote down the make, model, color, and the license plate number before sprinting to his own car with hopes of following them. He did, and was easily able to find out her name, where she lived, and after a few days of stalking her - where she worked, that she was single, had no roommate, and that the security of her apartment building was lacking.

What Mr. Orwell didn't understand was his place in the circle. I was, in fact, the Alpha predator, and as he stalked his prey, I did the same to him. All the while he was watching her, I was watching him, but the problem was, I am infinitely better at tracking.

When he finally decided to pull the trigger and kidnap her, I made a spur of the moment decision not to intercede at that time. I needed seclusion, not for rescuing her, but for what I planned to do to him after I set her free. My guess was he had a good place to take her, away from prying eyes, a place to enact his maniacal fantasy. I would use that location to turn the tables on him.

I remember it was raining that night and I ended up soaked to the bone. It made sneaking around easier, but I was so cold and that only worked on making me more and more pissed off as the night went on.

I stood in the rain between two buildings, hiding in the shadows. There were a couple of street lights along the sidewalk illuminating the whole area more than I would have liked. I'd have to be careful. I could easily end up the main suspect in a kidnapping or a murder if a bystander snapped a photo of me and the evening went sour. My car was nearby so I could bolt as soon as the target took off in his vehicle. I would use my hoodie to strategically obscure my face. I crossed my fingers and hoped it would be enough.

Mr. Orwell had studied Janelle's schedule and he knew on Thursday nights she would get home around 11:30. He knew the street would be mostly clear as there was rarely any foot traffic that late, and if he worked quick enough, he'd have no problem with his plan. I assumed he would have to take her on the street. I doubted she would have let him in the apartment. A risky move I never would have taken, too much potential for witnesses, but that's why I'm me and he's the fucking asshole he is.

Mr. Orwell parked his BMW right in front of her apartment and waited. He used the ol' reverse damsel in distress routine, something I duplicated the regular version of for my take down of the Battle Boys. I have no shame in using borrowed and road-tested techniques. If it works, it works, and one should not mess with what works.

He opened the hood of his car and pretended he was having car trouble. His hair was now slicked back and he was clean shaven. He wore an expensive suit that I was sure cost more than two grand. He was unrecognizable from when Janelle had last seen him, and his weird outfit at The Boardwalk suddenly made sense. This guy was wealthy, like doesn't connect with the general population kind of wealthy, the kind of man who believes that everyday people wear polos and khaki pants to an amusement park kind of wealthy. He had worn a disguise, though a poorly realized one, and for me, the entire situation became much more intriguing. Obviously, he was playing a much deeper game than I had imagined.

When Janelle came walking up the street at a steady pace, red umbrella in hand, Mr. Orwell put on a show involving his cell phone and a fake lack of signal. He laid it on thick as she walked by, mumbling outrage, holding his phone in the air in various positions. He didn't bother trying to stay out of the rain.

At first, she didn't react, but just as she turned to head up the steps to her front door, the Good Samaritan in her could not resist. She turned and took one step toward his car. "Having car troubles?"

He acted surprised and startled by her presence. "Oh, hi.

Yeah. Worked late and took a shortcut to get home faster and my damn car died. Now I can't get a signal to call triple A."

"Cell phones can be fickle around here. Mineral deposits." Janelle pulled her own phone from her purse and swiped the screen. "I'm getting two bars. What's the number? I'll call for you."

What happened next I did feel guilty about, as I could have prevented it, but I just couldn't chance it.

Mr. Orwell walked toward Janelle with his right arm out in front of him, the cell phone in his palm as if he were going to hand it over to her. So smooth that I barely even noticed myself, he used his left hand to remove a crowbar he had hidden near the engine of his car and he placed that arm straight down at his side.

Janelle didn't even see it coming.

Right in stride with his steps, Mr. Orwell cracked her on the side of the head with the crowbar just hard enough to make her bleed and knock her out, but not so hard as to crush her skull. He didn't want her dead, after all, he wanted her very much alive. How else would he enjoy her face as he violated her, the tears, the muffled screams?

Janelle flew to the side and crumbled to the ground like a sack of flour. The thud of the crowbar smacking her head and her body hitting the ground made me double-cringe.

I seized the opportunity to sneak over to my car, staying low to make sure I wouldn't be seen. Then again, Mr. Orwell was a little distracted.

He worked fast. First, he picked up Janelle's purse, cell phone, and umbrella, then he rushed over to his car, opened the back door, and threw the items and his crowbar onto the rear seat. He quietly shut the door and used his key fob to open the trunk. With pure brute strength, he hoisted Janelle from the ground doing a proper squat. He lumbered back to his car and carefully put her in the trunk, again shutting the door softly.

Playing it cool, he surveyed the area in all directions to make sure the coast was clear. Satisfied, he closed the hood of his car and got behind the wheel.

I squeezed the door handle of my car and pulled it open an inch at a time, praying the hinges wouldn't squeak. There was a minor grinding noise about halfway through but I don't think anyone further than five feet away could have heard it. I got in, slouching down still, only closing the door and starting the car once Mr. Orwell had driven off and was near the end of the block. I pulled away, stayed a good distance behind him, my headlights off.

He seemed to be in no hurry, better for me trying to keep up with him. Of course, he didn't want to get caught speeding or something while he had a woman in his trunk, and if I was a moron, I could've given him some credit for that, but fuck him.

The Chelsea Bay Marina was the biggest one in a three-county area and housed nearly one hundred fifty boats. Impressive place.

In my best Robin Leach voice, I said, "Lifestyles of the rich and famous, this is how they spend their summer weekends, on yachts worth more than the average American's house and cars combined. Lavish and decadent, many come equipped with hot tubs, caviar, and hundred dollar bills to use as toilet paper."

Don't get me wrong, I have no problem with wealth in general, but let's be real. Most of these assholes were either born into money or they got most of it by pushing paper or by cutting the legs out from under good, hardworking people who do all the work and barely get by. American dream, my ass.

I left my car a good distance away, my trusty backpack of supplies on my back and a few other items in my pockets, and jogged over to where he had parked. When I made eyes on him, I had to give him props. He put more thought into all this than I would have guessed him capable. Near his car, there was a large barrel-style garbage can, and hidden behind it was a collapsible wheelchair, which he brought to his car. He opened it up and placed Janelle's still unconscious body into the seat. I had wondered how he was going to get her from his car to their final destination, especially without being seen. Clever bastard.

The rain had let up but I was still trembling a bit from the chill. I wanted to be indoors, dry and warm. Janelle's life was on the line, however, so I knew I had to suck it up. I stayed back and watched Mr. Orwell through a tiny scope I often kept in my lower left cargo pants pocket. I'm amazed at the shit you can find on the interwebs. Spy cams the size of a button, GPS wrist watches, and an expandable monocular not much bigger than the size of a permanent marker.

He wheeled her down the main dock and split off to the left. Once he got to his boat, he made quick work of getting her inside. I didn't go after them immediately. I wanted to make sure he had time to get comfortable, let his guard down.

Ten minutes passed. I crouched low and made my way toward the boat. At spot C-19, I found a gorgeous yacht I would guess was just over fifty feet long, and the empty wheelchair sitting on the outer deck. As gently as I could so the boat would not rock, I snaked on board and stood at the small staircase leading down to the main cabin door. I centered myself, heartbeat at normal, breathing shallow and calm. Every possible scenario of attack and counter-attack ran through my head like a playbook I had studied for months. Boy, was he going to be surprised.

I wasted no time, not wanting Janelle to receive any further injury. I armed myself, a close contact stun gun in one hand, a jagged and vicious looking hunting knife in the other. I took the stairs down and carefully turned the doorknob to reveal it was unlocked. Brazenly, a woman on a mission, I threw open the door and burst into the room.

I surveyed the space briefly, for logistically purposes. The room was a combo living room, kitchen, and dining room, dimly lit but well kept, spotless actually. A narrow passage lay directly before me leading to the bedroom and bath.

I ran across the room, down the hallway, and into the bedroom, stopping at the foot of the bed where Janelle was completely naked on her back, arms tied to the headboard posts with thick nautical rope, her mouth covered in duct tape, her legs spread apart, each tied around the ankles with a tightly wound bedsheet, the other ends secured to the underside of the bedframe. Wide awake, her reddened eyes screamed for freedom, the side of her head where she had taken the crowbar was black and purple with bruising, her skin and hair around the area spattered in blood. She squirmed and mumbled. Bad idea. I shook my head and put my index finger to my lips, then turned to the bathroom. Thankfully, she heeded my warning.

I could hear the shower running, a fortunate advantage for me. I stepped to the doorway and peeked inside. That asshole was in the shower behind frosted glass, singing what sounded like a bad karaoke version of some eighties hair-metal song. His demeanor, his carefree fucking attitude really pissed me off in that moment. I wanted to cut his junk off and make him eat it before letting him bleed to death. I had it in me, I knew I did, but I'm no murderer. Exceptions can be made, I thought. I mean, come on, this guy is about to do some pretty awful shit to an innocent woman. She will almost certainly end up dead afterward, which might be months from now, who knows. Killing him would be justice, my civic duty, a favor to society.

I reached over to the vanity and picked up his toothbrush. I didn't want to try and take him down while he was in the shower, so I hid behind the bathroom door. Aiming carefully, I tossed his toothbrush at the glass shower door. It smacked right on target and fell to the floor.

The impact made him jump back. "Shit ... what the hell was that?" His chipper mood had suddenly turned scared, much to my delight.

He shut off the water and opened the shower door. Nothing appeared out of place until he stepped out and his left foot landed on his toothbrush. Confused, he bent over and picked it up, a look of wonder crossing his face. So arrogant in his plans, he blew off the incident by throwing the toothbrush in the sink. He used the only bath towel on the bar to dry off, then folded it and returned it exactly as it was.

He went to the mirror, so I lowered myself to avoid being seen in the reflection. He ran his hand over his face, turning his head from side to side, checking himself out. He then brushed his hair, pursed his lips, and checked out his face again like he was getting ready for a date.

Oh boy, I wanted to hurt him so bad. My fists were clenched so tight around the stun gun and hilt of the knife, my knuckles were red and starting to hurt.

Naked, he left the bathroom and returned to his captive. He licked his lips.

"Oh, honey. I'm probably going to enjoy this a helluva lot more than you will, but then ... you look like the dirty little whore type."

Clearly, this guy was on some kind of power trip. He was a relatively good looking guy, clearly successful in business, stone-cold rich. He could have his choice of trophy wives, or at least his pick of the highest class of escorts to use for his sick fantasies. This was something more, not about sex, not about power even. My best guess, he's just bored and happens to be lacking any humanity. A good and decent person could never do what he has done, is about to do. I think when someone like Mr. Orwell runs out of things and people to buy, he must get a thrill from something forbidden. I've heard of cases where a group of rich brats kill a homeless man or some frat boys rape and kill a trick. They feel like they're above the fray, better than others. Whatever his deal was, I intended to end it.

I emerged from behind the door and got to about two feet behind him. I wanted to see the look on his face when he realized I was there, so I tapped his shoulder with the tip of my knife blade.

He jerked and popped around to face me, his eyes wide with surprise. He tried to speak but I didn't want to hear another word from his disgusting mouth, so I put the stun gun to his chest and let him have fifty thousand volts of juice that instantly put him on the floor with a squeal. I decided to bring along a close contact stunner as I knew the quarters would be cramped and I didn't want to take a chance.

While keeping a close eye on him, I hurried over to Janelle and removed her bindings. She peeled the duct tape off her own face. I tossed her clothes to her.

"Get dressed. I'll take you home shortly."

She grabbed her underwear and with shaky hands, pulled them on in a fumbling panic.

I looked over to her. "You're going to be okay."

She didn't respond or look back at me. Tears streamed from her eyes as she struggled to get her bra and top on.

I don't tend to be overly emotional, so I wasn't sure what to say to help her calm down. I thought about what I would want to help me relax in a stressful situation, and then it came to me.

"Wanna hurt him?"

She didn't answer immediately.

I glanced down to Mr. Orwell. He was getting clear, fast. Time for action.

"Janelle?"

"I wanna go home," she finally answered.

"We need to teach this yucko a lesson." I rolled Mr. Orwell to his side and used the sheets he had used to tie up Janelle to secure his arms behind his back and lock his ankles together. "You may not even be the first person he's done this to. He's a rich prick and we need to make sure he doesn't do this shit again."

"I can't."

"Look, I understand this has been ... traumatic, I do, and believe me, you'll have plenty of time to cry over this and be scared, but right now," I put a little authoritative tone on the final part, "I need you to get tough."

She burst into tears and put her in face in her hands.

I walked over to the bedside.

"Janelle, you're safe now." I put a hand on her upper back. "I promise I'll make sure you never see this asshole again, but to do that, we need to hurt him. Guys like him only understand extremes. So, for this, we have no choice but to go there."

She looked up to me. "Can't you just," she pointed to the knife holstered on my waist, "take care of him?"

"No. We can't kill him. We'd never be able to stop running from something like that. And trust me, it won't really help. I know what I'm talking about."

She had calmed down some by that point and we locked eyes.

"Just take a deep breath and I'll start."

She did as I asked.

I came around to the end of the bed and grabbed Mr. Orwell, shifting him upward to a sitting position against the end of the bed. He was recovering and starting to wiggle around. The smell of urine hit my nose hard. There was a puddle next to him on the floor, an occasional side effect of stunning someone.

"You say one fuckin' word and I'll use this blade to cut out your tongue," I threatened with a stern glare.

I waved Janelle over and she came around to the foot of the bed but stayed a good five feet from Mr. Orwell.

"Now watch." I bent my knees and stood slightly turned to the right, my best version of a karate stance, my fists in the air, the left higher than the right. With every ounce of power I could muster, I made the first one count and plowed Mr. Orwell in the side of the head with a right hook. His head jerked sideways. Janelle winced at the thud.

"God damn it!" shouted Mr. Orwell. "You bitch!"

"Hey! What did I say about talking?"

"You hit me!"

I unsheathed my knife and poked the tip into his Adam's apple.

He lifted his chin and shut his mouth.

"You hit her with a crowbar you sick fuck. One more peep," I said as I pushed the knife in ever so slightly, "and you lose your voice box." I released the blade. "Nod if you understand me."

He gave me two quick ones.

I put the knife away and took the bag off my back and unzipped it. I removed a telescoping rod, extended it, and handed the weapon to Janelle.

With reluctance, she took it.

"How is this going to teach him anything?" Janelle asked.

"Trust me. Take one good swing at him and I'll show you exactly why you'll never see him again. He was going to rape you, probably for days or weeks. Do it!"

I could see the anger building in her.

"He wouldn't hesitate for one second to hurt you. Now do it!"

Rage filled her eyes.

"He smashed you in the head with a crowbar and tied you naked to a bed while he enjoyed a nice, hot shower."

She made eye contact with Mr. Orwell. In that moment, she saw in his eyes the same deviant I had witnessed at the pier. Her blood boiled.

A primal scream emerged from Janelle's lips that almost scared me for a second, but I understood. She had to dig deep to do what she was about to do. She had probably never physically hurt another human being in her whole life. I did it all the time. I had actually gotten a little too comfortable with it, to be honest.

Janelle took one step forward and with a wide swing, whipped the baton through the air, making full contact with her captor's right cheek and lips. The hit tore up his face good. Blood sprayed across his arm and onto the floor. Unexpectedly, Janelle stepped even closer and started hitting him over and over with smaller strokes, making contact with every part of his body visibly available to her. She released a high-pitched yelp with each hit. Mr. Orwell groaned and winced and recoiled but made no major outbursts.

Once out of breath, she stepped back, threw the baton down, and collapsed to her knees, crying.

I pulled a tablet computer from my bag and turned it on. I

opened a folder of pictures and clicked on the first one before showing the screen to Mr. Orwell, who by that time could only see out of his right eye. The other one was bruised, bloody, and sealed shut by the swelling.

The image revealed Mr. Orwell standing at the bathroom door on the Boardwalk as Janelle left the public bathroom. The next photo showed him clearly following her out to the parking lot. One by one, I revealed all the pics to him and then to Janelle. They showed him watching her come home from work on a few different days, and then one of him standing at his car as she arrived home on that very same night. The final one of him pushing Janelle down the dock in a wheelchair really sealed the deal because even through the damage to his face, I could tell he understood how fucked he was.

"Now let me educate you, Mr. Orwell, about the next critical steps in your evolution. I'm sending these photos to a few trusted friends for safekeeping. Should anything bad happen to either Janelle or myself, EVER, they will be published and your life will effectively be over. Nod if you understand me."

He did.

"I'm also going to be keeping a very close eye on you, and if I even get the faint odor of you mistreating a woman, I will use this knife to castrate you. Nod if you understand me."

He did.

"Good. Now you may be wondering, why are we not just going to call the police and put you in prison? Simple. A delicate little flower like you would die in prison, and you can't financially compensate Janelle here if you're dead. You will give her two thousand dollars a month, every month, until I tell you to stop. I'll give you details for these monthly transactions at a later date. Nod if you understand me."

He hesitated.

I gave him a ruthless backhand to the right side of his face.

He spat mucus and blood to his left, then nodded in compliance.

"My fee, of course, is I keep your fuckin' boat. And you're not allowed to come anywhere near this marina. Any violations and the pics go out and you go to jail, but before that, I kick your ass again and certain parts of you will not go to prison with you. Nod if you understand me."

He wept as he nodded. "I'm sorry," he mumbled with a bloody and swelling mouth. Sobbing, he said again, "I'm sorry."

"No asshole! You don't get to be sorry. You didn't make a mistake, this wasn't an accident. This was calculated and demonic. So, you don't get to apologize. It doesn't mean shit. What you get is punishment, and with that, hopefully, no one else will ever get hurt by you again. You're sorry you got caught. So, fuck your sorrys. Now shut up."

I spotted two sets of keys sitting on the end table, so I grabbed them both and put them in my pocket. I needed a new place to shack up and the boat would be perfect.

I used my knife to cut the sheet from around his feet.

"Get up," I commanded, grabbing his arm to assist. "Time for you to go home." I looked to Janelle who had gotten to her feet and was busy putting her shoes on. "Find his wallet, take all the money, but hang on to the wallet." I scanned the room. "It's on the dresser." I pointed. "Follow us out, okay?"

Janelle found four hundred dollars in cash in the wallet, stuffed the bills in her pocket, and was right behind me as I guided Mr. Orwell out of the cabin and onto the deck.

On the dock, I sat his ass naked in the wheelchair.

"What are you going to do with me?" Mr. Orwell asked.

"You don't get to talk," I answered. I yanked on his hair hard enough for him to get the message.

I pushed him down the docks, the planks still wet from the rain, Janelle in tow, until we arrived at his car. I dropped his wallet and car keys in his lap.

"Get in your car. Go straight home. Take a few days to think about all this."

He rose from the wheelchair, stumbling a bit, almost dropping his keys. He found and pressed the UNLOCK button on his key fob and approached the door. He wanted the night to be over with just as bad as Janelle and I.

I collapsed the wheelchair and shoved it into the backseat of his car.

Mr. Orwell climbed behind the wheel like an elderly man, slow, in pain.

I came to him. "I'll be contacting you soon. Have two thousand, cash, available in the next seventy-two hours. Remember everything I've told you. I'm not fucking around. At some point in the coming weeks or months, you're going to start thinking too hard about ways to get out of this situation, but let me assure, every effort will end in the same result. DO NOT ... fuck with me."

No response was necessary, so I shut the car door and off he went. He peeled out as he exited the lot.

I took Janelle home but we didn't exchange a single word on the ride home. She simply stared out of the side window into the darkness. The confusion and pain she must have been pondering, it broke my heart.

I parked directly in front of her building.

"Everything's going to be fine now. You won't see him again." I paused. It would be a process for her. She wasn't going to grasp everything right away. She sure as hell wasn't going to feel safe for a while.

"I'll check in on you frequently."

"Why didn't you stop him?" Janelle asked.

Confused, I asked, "How do you mean?"

"The pictures," she said.

Suddenly, I understood.

"If you were watching him watching me that whole time, why didn't you stop him from taking me in the first place?" She was getting angry.

There was no explanation I could have given her that would satisfy, not so soon after.

"He was never going to stop unless I got him in the act. I'm sorry for that, I really am."

"He could have killed me."

"I was never going to let that happen. I'm sorry you were injured. Trust me though, had it not gotten as far as it did, we'd have had no leverage, and in six months he'd be doing this shit again. Try not to think about all that right now. You need to rest."

She relented but did not seem completely satisfied, which I expected. She rubbed her eyes and nodded. "I'm so tired. I just need to go to bed."

I doubted she would actually sleep, and even if she somehow managed to, her nightmares would raise her in a cold sweat, screaming, flailing. There would be no easy way past her trauma.

"I'll call you in a couple of days and we'll talk more."

"Thank you ... for saving me. I don't mean to sound ungrateful." She sobbed with a hand to her mouth.

"Don't worry about it," I said, shaking my head. "Now go on. Get some rest. And don't tell anyone about what happened. Just say you fell and hit your head on a coffee table or something, if anyone should inquire."

"Okay." She opened her door and left the vehicle.

Once I witnessed her enter the apartment and shut the door behind her, I sped off.

The coffee shop, Grind Me, is on the corner of 11th Avenue and East Monroe. Busy place, good vanilla latte, not my crowd, but Janelle works nearby and feels comfortable there. This will be our third in-person meeting since the incident. I have already given her the first two-thousand-dollar payment from Mr. Orwell, the second one arrived as scheduled in my postal box, and I plan to give it to her today.

I enter the coffee shop and find her sitting at a table near the back, close to the door that reads EMPLOYEES ONLY, just as I had requested. Occupational hazard. I prefer to face the main entrance when possible and she obliged. I sit down to discover she has ordered me a coffee.

"This for me?"

"Of course," Janelle answers.

We talk between sips of coffee and my occasional scanning of the room and all the people coming and going.

"Thank you. How you been?"

"Getting better with each day. I stopped looking over my shoulder every second."

"That's good."

"But every time I see a Beemer like his, I kind of panic." Her breathing is heavier just mentioning it.

"That's understandable. The shit I've been through, I rarely rest easy. It'll get better for ya. Believe it or not, not every person in the world is out to get you. You were just a bit unlucky. Wrong time and place." I slide the envelope across the table.

She places her hand on it but pauses.

"What is it?" I ask.

"You must be rubbing off on me, but that fancy pants lady over by the front window, I could swear she keeps looking over here at us."

My interest piqued, I throw eyes in the direction of the front window. A sharply dressed woman, maybe forty-five years old and wearing a pants suit sits alone, a magazine in one hand, a clear cup in the other hand containing some disgusting looking green liquid. She indeed looks our way, multiple times, with subtle peeks.

"And," she dithers some before continuing, "I don't think I want this money."

I hear her but don't process the words. I am already too busy being fixated on the mystery woman. Based on her appearance, she could be a lawyer, perhaps in finance, maybe a realtor, but that's pushing it. I'm pretty sure her shoes cost more than I spent last year on food.

I stop for a second and think about what Janelle had just said.

"What?" I ask.

"The money, I don't think I want anymore. It feels dirty."

She's right. It's filthy money and a reminder of a situation I'm sure she'd just as soon forget. Two payments in, however, just didn't seem like enough reparations. The upside of stopping the money is the paper trail disappearing. Every interaction has risks. Every meeting, every call, every mail drop. Risk, risk, risk.

"I get it. I can stop them if you want, but take this last one. I mean, hell, he already gave it up."

She picks up the envelope and stuffs it in her purse.

"Okay, but please, no more after this. I have to admit, part of me thinks he should go to jail."

I figured this was coming. "Only problem is, he barely did anything that would warrant much jail time. Assault, kidnapping. That's about it. When he got out of prison, he'd just be more pissed and we'd lose our leverage."

"That's true. I guess I never thought about it like that."

"Yeah, and trust me, he's never going to try anything like that again. We may be saving other potential victims."

"I know. Part of me just feels like justice hasn't been fully served."

"Sure. But someday, his true reckoning will come, not sure what that is, but it will come. Keep taking the money. It might do you some good down the line."

"All right."

"Everything else going well? Work, boyfriends?"

"Work is fine. And no, no boyfriends. I can't even look most men in the eye right now."

"Don't let that a-hole do that to you. He is not any kind of example of men in general. He's a rotten apple in an otherwise healthy orchard."

"Maybe."

I notice the strange woman rise up and make her way toward the exit, so I decide I need to investigate. I can never be too careful.

"I need to run, Janelle. Go buy yourself something expensive. Or donate some money to an animal shelter." I rise from my seat and take one final swig of my coffee. "You'll feel better."

"Thanks again, Josey, for everything, just in case I haven't told you enough. I'm so thankful for what you did."

I nod. "I'll see you in about a month." I look to the exit. The woman is two steps out. "I gotta go. Bye."

I rush away from the table without a response, navigating the afternoon crowd of fellow caffeine addicts. By the time I hit the sidewalk outside, the woman has reached a large black SUV on 11th Avenue, about twelve spots down from the coffee shop. She gets in the backseat of the vehicle, which comes off as odd, so I decide to venture in her direction even though I probably shouldn't.

I walk down the sidewalk, slowly, my phone in hand so I can pretend to be in a casual conversation with someone.

I mouth words into the phone but as I got closer, I actually starting verbalizing a fake conversation.

"Well Jesus, Vanessa, how many times are you gonna let that jackass do that to you?"

Vanessa does not reply.

"That's just wrong, so wrong."

Vanessa is so quiet, I'm not sure she exists.

At the SUV, the rear windows are all tinted so I can't get a good look inside. There is no one in the front seats. I keep walking. Five feet past, I hear a car door open and a voice emerges.

"Miss Baldwin. I'd like to have a word with you."

Stunned at hearing my last name, something very few people on the whole planet know, I stop and turn to find the rear passenger side door of the SUV open. Just then, my back muscles tense at the pressure from a gun barrel in my spine.

"Don't turn around." The man pushes his gun a bit harder into my back for emphasis. "We'd like to have a chat. Walk, slowly to the SUV and get in. Any sudden movements and your insides become your outsides." The man's deep voice is mesmerizing.

I doubt he would kill me right on the street, although, I don't know who I'm dealing with, so better safe than sorry. It's my own damn fault. Didn't keep a close enough eye on my surroundings as I investigated. Classic trap and I fell for it.

Idiot!

I enter the backseat to find the woman from the coffee shop. She appears completely at ease. I don't think she realizes how close I am to throat-chopping her and making a run for it. I also get a glimpse of the man as he shuts the door. I swear I've seen him somewhere before, and then it dawns on me. The tall, black man in the suit on Harris. I knew it. Damn it. I need to learn to trust my instincts more. Save me a ton of trouble.

The man runs around to the driver's side and gets in the front seat before turning the gun back on me.

"I don't think we need that anymore," the woman assures her partner.

He keeps his eyes locked on me but holsters his weapon.

"Do you know who we are, Josey? Can I call you that?" the woman asks, very cordially.

"I'm not sure it really matters what you call me. And no, I have no idea who you are, but I don't feel particularly inclined to be open with you considering you've been spying on me for weeks and just had a gun in my back."

"Madame K was right. You're even keener than some of us thought. My name is Dina and this is Ollie. We're part of an organization that secures," she pauses to choose her words carefully, "a certain kind of contract for special services, and then executes those special services for a price."

"Contract assassination. You could have just said that. I'm not an idiot." I give her a face of incredulity. Mockingly, I say, "Yeah, and I'm the sanitation specialist for the Hyatt Companies. No, you're a janitor at a hotel, asshole."

"You're a smartass," Ollie finally joins the conversation. Even insulting me, I could listen to that voice all day. I turn to him. "You ever do radio? You have a great voice, soothing even." He probably thinks I'm being snarky but I'm dead serious.

"Don't be rude, Ollie. She's our guest."

"So, if I'm your guest, I can leave then, right?"

"Absolutely, but I think you'll want to hear us out."

"I see one of two situations happening here. One, someone hired you to take me out, in which case, I'd probably be dead already so we'll rule that out. Or two, you want to hire me, and in that case, fuck you and have a nice day. Can I go now?"

"Hire you? Not quite!" Dina almost cackles. "There are protocols for working in our rarified vocation. We have a school, an academy of sorts where we evaluate and train would be contract professionals. Very few people have the necessary skills for such a thing, but our initial assessment of you is quite favorable and we'd like to see just how capable you are."

"Pass," I say with as much disinterest in my voice as I can muster.

"Don't you get tired of hitting up small timers like the Battle Boys just to get by? That's too easy for you, well beneath your skill level. This would be an opportunity to make a real difference in this often-complicated world, a world full of discourse and evil and guys like James Orwell. That's all small potatoes."

I feel violated. How long have they been watching me? Much longer than I realize. The Leer family crosses my mind, and their dad. Have they been watching me that long? Do they know what happened to him? What I did? I start to get nervous.

I shake my head. "Pass."

"Did I mention the money? It wouldn't take long before you could buy five of those boats like the one you live in. And the Leers, you could make sure little Evie can go to any college she wants to, and maybe buy them a new house too. Wouldn't that be nice?"

Fuck. Looks like these guys have done their homework. If they know about the Leers, it stands to reason they know enough to make my life a living hell, should they choose to. I try hard to keep a neutral facial expression, even though on the inside, I'm molten lava.

"There's so much risk in doing what you do. With our

training and methods, you'll be doing basically the same thing, except in a much more controlled way, with better resources, access to things you've never even heard of, and ... you'll never have to worry about money ever again."

"Killing people is not," I throw up air quotes, "basically the same thing. I do what I have to do to get by. I don't end people. That's very permanent, ya know?"

"Do you really believe that the world would not be a better place if a few individuals here and there were taken out, for the greater good?"

"You mean for money?"

"Well, yes, we are well paid, but the money is not the why. The why is because there needs to exist a balance in the world, and people like you and me and Ollie understand the deck is stacked, and sometimes the playing field must be leveled and this is one way to do that. It just happens to be highly lucrative."

"She lives in a stolen boat and drives a turd of a car, Dina," Ollie adds. "I don't think she cares that much about riches."

"But she does care about people, and ultimately, what we do is help people. Look, all we're asking is for you to come visit the academy, take a few tests, and see what you think. If after all that, you still decide to pass, fine. But please allow us to show you, not just tell you, what we're all about."

I still don't feel like I have much choice for some reason. They held just short of threatening me with all that Leer talk and what they may or may not know about it. Doesn't mean they wouldn't at some point. I don't like people having something they can hold over me. The last time I discovered such control over me, it ended with nothing but bad. When backed into a corner, I'm capable of anything.

Dina hands me a business card. I don't even look at it.

"In forty-eight hours, we'd like you to join us for a one day evaluation. After which, you will be either invited to join the academy for a more intensive training program, or you can go back to your life as it exists today. Your choice."

"I'll think about it. Can I go now?"

"You may. Call the number to get instructions on where to go. I sincerely hope to see you again, Josey."

I say nothing else and bolt, running full speed down the block to my car. I jump behind the wheel and pull away as fast as possible. I need to clear my head, so I drive out of town, and once out in the open, I fly at near ninety miles an hour to let loose some adrenaline. Twenty miles out I hit a rest stop and pull off to use the bathroom and walk around. I exit the car and walk the long sidewalk up to the building.

My head spins with questions and worries. They knew about the Leer kids. I can only assume they know about Wayne Leer. I become sick to my stomach and bend over, relieving myself of what little contents are in my stomach. Mostly spoiled latte. I wipe my mouth on my sleeve, take in some deep breaths, and make my way to the restroom. I splash some water on my face and drink a handful to clear the acid from my mouth. I pee, wash my hands, and leave, taking the long path back to my car. The air of the country is nice, clean. It's easy to forget how nasty the city air can be. You get used to it. Only once you leave does it become so apparent.

I figure it won't hurt to check out the place. How long can I expect to scrape by the way I do? Maybe it's time to think about the future. And, she made a good point about Evie and taking care of them. It pisses me off that she tried to use that shit against me, but damn it, she might be right.

I'm simply not confident I can kill someone, even some really awful motherfucker, except in defense of myself or someone I care about. But that money. Might be some Hollywood money there. I can finally get out of this shit-hole town and live a better life. Hard to admit, but that would be sweet.

My head hurts. I need food, and a distraction. Time to head back to town and take in a movie with popcorn, a box of chocolates, nachos, and a big ass soda. Not food I would normally consume, but today has not been a normal day.

# 6

Tuesday Evening

I'm sitting in bed on the yacht. It's just after dark. I can't relax. Every time I hear any sound - water sloshing, boats creaking, dock boards warping - my heart jumps awake, my blood surging with adrenaline. I assume they're still watching me. I don't much like being the target of surveillance. I have no idea how the hell I'm going to sleep from now on. Fuck!

I still haven't looked at the business card. Normal human curiosity is compelling me to give it a shot. No harm in checking into it. Of course, no matter what I decide to do, I have to move again, get another car, and find a way to do those things without the watchful eyes of this Kill Academy place. Not going to be easy.

I slide the business card from the nightstand and lay eyes on the details of it for first time, or more accurately the lack of details. I flip the card front to back twice, scowling at the damn thing. Both sides are completely blank.

"Is this a joke?" I ponder the notion of giving someone a blank business card and what the point would be. I quickly surmise their need for discretion.

"It's a test. Now I just have to figure it out."

I rub the side of my face, staring all the while at the card. I flip it from one side to the other, holding it under the light, at different angles, blowing hot breathe on it. Nothing.

Now on a mission, I hop from bed and take it to the kitchen. I walk to the refrigerator and open the freezer. I suspend the card directly in the center and wait for a minute, hoping the cold air would trigger some temperature sensitive ink. No text appears.

I think back to what Dina had said when she handed it to me. I was so focused on getting out of her car, I worry I hadn't paid close enough attention to her words.

I close my eyes and try to take my mind back. I listen hard for her voice. I hear it. *Call the number to get instructions on where to go.*

I believe that's what she said. Not terribly helpful.

I suddenly remember seeing a t-shirt the last time I went shopping where the print glows in the dark. I bet that's it.

I have damn near every light on in the boat tonight, so I go to the smallest room, the bathroom, shut the door behind me, and flick the light switch off. I wait with the card held in front of my face. I flip the card to the other side. I don't see anything. Suddenly, a faint change appears in soft yellow. Sure enough, a ten-digit phone number is on the card. Clever. I turn it back over to find nothing. I read the number aloud ten times to get it stuck in my brain before exiting the bathroom to find my phone.

I punch the number in and just stare at it on the screen. I still can't determine whether I'm truly interested in the opportunity or whether I'll be calling because I feel threatened to do so. I loathe the idea of that last part. I'd be better off just running away, to another town, another life, another line of work. I have a million reasons to go away, really only one to stay. But that one...

I hover my right index finger over the CALL button and notice my hand is trembling. I'm not sure if the cause is nervousness over the prospect of something new and exciting or the kind where my instincts are telling me to run away as fast as I can. I think I want to hurl, but I still press the screen and put the phone to my ear.

There are a series of strange clicks on the other end and then one ring.

"Please listen carefully as this message will play only once. This coming Thursday, please go, alone, to the corner of Hudson Street and Merriman Avenue. A late model, black SUV will arrive at precisely 11:15 pm. Enter the backseat of the vehicle. You will be blindfolded and taken to the training facility. You are allowed to bring three things: yourself, the clothes on your back, and your cell phone. The phone will be confiscated upon entering the vehicle and will be returned when you are dropped back off. All other items will be seized and destroyed."

I hear a click and the line goes dead.

I bring up a note-taking app on my phone and enter the details of the call, just in case. If I intend to follow through on this, I don't want to fuck up the first simple instructions they give me.

I know that area of town, it's not far from the seedy parts I frequent, and it's isolated.

"Not a bad place to snatch someone off the street and make them disappear."

I hear the words as the come out of my mouth and it dawns on me how paranoid I sound, not that I don't have cause to be, but it's tiresome. If I think these feelings are at a high now, I can only imagine how they might manifest as a contract killer. I'm betting the average assassin, even as coldhearted as one might think that kind of person could be, is either a borderline alcoholic or a hell-bent user of high grade pharmaceuticals. I doubt yoga, meditation, or any other mental exercises would be enough to keep those monsters in the mind cage.

# 7

Thursday

I spent all day Wednesday streaming rom-coms and independent films on the boat. Based on my personality, no one would guess those two movie genres would be up my alley, but I have enough thrills and blood in my life to fill ten lifetimes, so I don't need anymore. I enjoy the stupidity of the average romantic comedy and the genuine emotion and storytelling of independent films.

I'm not proud of it but I will admit to eating an entire bag of cheese puffs and a dozen bakery-fresh chocolate chip cookies. Not all at once, mind you, but a person can watch a shit-ton of movies in one day, and well ... snacks.

Today I can't think of anything else except my upcoming covert Kill Academy tour and testing. Every thirty minutes or so, I either completely convince myself I should go, or just the opposite, decide entirely to stay away.

My legs dangle from the dock edge as I look out to the bay. I'm facing east so the sun is setting behind me, but the bay is still quite gorgeous at this time of day. The water stages from a cornflower blue to something closer to midnight blue by the time the light dies off. The transformation is so subtle I almost don't notice it. The sky above runs endless, soft, and clear.

The beautiful scenery helps give me some perspective. I know I'm still young and have plenty of time to figure out my life going forward, but I have no idea the direction I should head to get what I want. Hell, I don't even know what I want. I'm a planner, a woman of details, but when it comes to my future, I'm blinded by the here and now. My basic survival takes so much of my time and energy, there's nothing left. The only argument Dina made that has compelled me in the least is the one of my future. Let's be real, there are only so many times I can slap the Battle Boys around and expose the utter stupidity of the other local lowlifes before I exhaust my streams of revenue. I suppose this thirty minute block of time counts as a big thumbs up for going. I think I'll just leave it at that and go take a long, hot shower and get a nap in before it's time to leave for my secret rendezvous.

I show up fifteen minutes early to the pickup spot. I see no one else while I wait, which could be good, could be bad. There used to be a small strip mall and a large department store down here, but when the department store closed, it eventually took everything else with it. Now there's just a title loan place on the far western edge of the strip mall and a giant parking lot full of shattered chunks of asphalt and potholes big enough to swallow a Prius.

I stand right on the corner, feeling a little like a prostitute minus the provocative clothes, uncomfortable high heels, and overdone makeup. I generally don't get nervous energy but right now I'm twiddling my fingers with anxiety. Evie's sweet little face pops into my head and it calms me. She's a good kid, rambunctious like I was at her age. The thought of her dad enters my mind and the serenity disappears as quickly as it had arrived. The truth eats at me, unbearably so. I need to rip the damn bandage off and give them the full story. They'll probably hate me and I'll lose the only family I've ever had. My omission is unforgivable. I'm sure they will see it that way. I hate myself for what I've done to them.

Like a perfectly timed lull in a rainstorm as one leaves the house, a black SUV snaps to a stop in front of me.

I whisper, barely moving my lips, "It's just a tour, Josey. Even after that, you can still walk away. Maybe they'll surprise you."

I leave all my apprehension on the sidewalk. I need to appear confident, fearless. I doubt they will have any use for an angst-filled, hand-shaking, nervous ball of fear kind of recruit. I shake it all loose and get in the vehicle.

I'm alone in the backseat. There is a driver. That is all. I've never seen him before. He turns to me and throws a velvety black hood in my lap. Then he leans over and picks up a couple of items from the passenger seat. He hands me a tiny bottle of what looks like water.

"Drink the entire bottle, then put the hood on, covering your entire face," the driver commands.

I understand the caution but I ask anyway, "Is this necessary?"

Without missing a beat and a little agitated, he says, "Do it or get the fuck out of the car. I'm not going to ask again." He turns and faces forward, watching me in his rearview mirror.

I react with my best alley-cat snarl and do as instructed. These people are not screwing around. I twist open the bottle and take a quick sniff. No odor. I assume it has something in it that will either knock me out or at least put me in a state of limited memory. I down it with two big gulps. I throw the bottle on the floor. I inspect the hood and see no discernable front, so I throw it over my head and lean back.

I remember sitting in the backseat for a few minutes without the driver pulling away. I remember feeling super drowsy and fighting the weight of my eyelids.

Flash forward and I'm on a twin bed with crisp white sheets, a single pillow, and a brown cotton blanket. The tiny room, not much bigger than the average single occupancy jail cell, is well lit. There is no toilet, no sink, no prison bars, no windows. Just the bed, a nightstand with a lamp and an alarm clock, and a regular door.

The green digits on the clock show 7:12 am. I can't believe they knocked me out for eight hours. I sit up and throw my legs over the edge of the bed. My head hurts so I rub my forehead. I need a coffee and an aspirin. Where the hell is this place?

From an unknown source, a bell much like a grade school class bell rings for five seconds. If I had been asleep, I sure as hell wouldn't be now. A few seconds later, the door to my room opens and Dina appears.

"So glad you decided to come, Josey. Follow me please. We're offering up some breakfast for the recruits before we get started today. I can imagine you'll need some caffeine, maybe something for the headache?"

"What was that shit you gave me?" I say as I rub the back of my head.

"Effective." Dina offers no more and leaves the room.

I rise from the bed and do some mild stretching, my shoulder aching per the usual. There's a small mirror on the wall. I use it to get a look at my hair on the way out. I run my fingers through it but it doesn't help much. Hell, I've seen it worse. I exit the room and see Dina to my right at the end of a short hallway. There are seven other people with her. Two more emerge from other rooms and follow me to the crowd.

"Oh good, you're all here. Welcome to orientation. I'm Dina, though I know we've all met. We're going to have a little breakfast before we get started today. Make sure you eat something, you'll need the brain power. At eight o'clock, you'll be given an exam that takes about ninety minutes, then each group will get a tour of the facility, as well as a chance to meet some of the instructors."

All of us recruits glance around at one another, sizing each other up in case we get to pick our groups. First impressions, I'd say a few of these fellas do not look suited one bit for the life of an assassin, but I know better than to judge a book by its cover. I assume my physical appearance will be underestimated as well, and those opinions will be dead wrong. I feel confident I can kick the shit out of at least six of these guys. I say guys, but one of my pick-six is the only other female of the ten of us. That's disappointing.

Dina puts a quick end to my group choosing theory. "And just so you're all aware, the groups I mentioned are really two completely different sets of training recruits. If the five of you that are here for Tech Ops could please head down the hallway to the last door on the right and get some food, I need to have a word with the others. Thank you." She holds out an arm and ushers them away.

My instincts were correct. Five of the six recruits I had pinned as oddballs have turned out to be here, not for assassin training, but for Tech Ops. Nerds is what they are. And that's a good thing. A few of them look like they haven't seen the sun in months. And believe me, I mean no disrespect to the computer whizzes and gamers of the world, at least not the socially functioning ones. I'm really referring to the near cave-dwelling, barely disconnected from the Matrix, desperately needing to go see a live concert and remember what it's like to be truly alive again type. Can't be much of a life when your entire experience with the world is done in cyberspace or in your own head. The inside of my mind is fucked up. If I spent too much time in there, it would not be pretty.

The Tech Ops candidates walk away and when out of earshot, Dina addresses us. "I know it will be easy to get into a pissing contest with one another, but keep in mind, this is not a competition. Any or all of you can make it. Will some of you fail? Yes. Statistically, most of you will not succeed here. But that will not be because one of you is better or worse. It will be based on your own individual successes and failures. Just keep that in mind."

Dina has incredible insight as a psychologist or she's just done this so many times she can see the signs. I'm guessing she's playing a little reverse psychology, sparking us to up our games through competitive behavior by telling us it's unnecessary. Clever. Reverse challenge accepted.

Dina leads us to the dining hall. She points to a buffet-style setup with the works. We funnel to the area and form a line. The tomboy in me tries to get the guys to go ahead of me but none of them are having it, insisting the lady get her food first. I acquiesce to their urgings. I want all of them to get the exact wrong impression about me. This will be a good start.

I stare at all the food and my headache is making it difficult to want anything but coffee. I see a blueberry muffin and figure I can probably nibble on it with a cup of joe. I grab a tray, a napkin-wrapped bundle of silverware, a blueberry muffin from a large basket full of them, and finish off with two twelve-ounce foam cups of coffee. I decide to take it black, getting my sugar from the muffin.

The room is brightly lit with daylight LED can lights, the walls a pale yellow, the floors a blue speckled gray restaurant grade, low-pile carpet. I still have yet to see a window. I would guess we are in the underground part of a building. That would make sense, considering the nature of this place.

There are four eight-foot long tables, each with six chairs. The Tech Ops recruits are at the table furthest from the entrance, chatting as they eat and drink, seeming like long, lost friends. They have something in common, of course - hacker stuff. I wonder what the rest of us will bond over - our lifelong morally ambiguous natures, how tough we are, how big our GEAR is. Of course, I'm a woman so I lack the basic framework, though I would guess I can make up for it with my street smarts.

I take a seat at the end of the table nearest the nerds so I can listen in on their conversations. The rest of my crew quickly filter around. An odd tension surrounds us and the talking stops once we're all in place, the silence broken only by the sounds of sipping, silverware clanking, and the occasional sniff.

"No reason this has to be awkward. You all heard Dina. This isn't a competition. We should get to know one another," one of the assassin recruits says in between the bites of his breakfast – a heaping pile of scrambled eggs and about ten strips of bacon. He chose water to drink.

Fucking Boy Scout. Probably was. He's grizzled, tanned, average height, muscular, I would guess just back from his last tour of duty in some god forsaken desert. Toughness factor, I'd guess he's a ten. Brains, well, we shall see.

"I mean, come on, there's no reason we can't all be friends and work together," he says. "And I'm Vick, by the way."

And there I have my answer. Well, he might not be dumb, perhaps he's just naïve. The military background would make sense, teamwork and all that.

The guy next to me speaks up. "Marcus. Good to meet you guys."

The introductions go on but I float my concentration to the other team. I don't hear every word but what I do is interesting. A male voice, "... hacked ... financial ... Bank of ... never found ..." A female voice, "City of ... grid ... resulted ... blackout ... used ... Wi-Fi ... breach."

I sense a stillness at my own table and can't pull my attention away from the others, then suddenly, I get a soft elbow from Marcus.

I give him my best 'what the fuck, dude?' look and notice everyone at the table is staring at me. Apparently, it's my turn, and here I am off in Neverland. These guys are going to think I'm an absentminded ditz. Good. Underestimate me all you want boys.

"Deep in thought?" Vick asks.

I nod, diffidently. "I'm Josey."

"Well, Josey, what's your story?" Vick probes.

"Not much to tell. Lifelong Christian right-winger with sociopathic tendencies, disassociate identity. Killed a kitten once."

Everyone at both tables stops talking and is now staring me down like we've all known that one of us is an alien in a human suit and they've just discovered I'm the fucking alien. I don't like the attention, the unfamiliar eyes on me, the judgments. Every damn one of these idiots looks like they're about to shit a brick, so I decide to finally let them off the hook.

I offer up a huge smile and start to laugh, pointing at Vick. "Haha! Got ya."

Vick smiles back. Eventually, everyone has a laugh, some of them nervously. I'm throwing so many mixed signals out there, no one is going to know where the hell I'm coming from when I speak.

"You're fuckin' hilarious," Marcus says. "You had me going there for a minute."

"I gotta keep you boys on your toes."

The casual background checks continue with no contribution from me. The groups keep to themselves which I don't really understand. I can see no reason why both sides shouldn't develop relationships because at some point the contract killers will be utilizing the Tech Ops people to complete missions - at least that would be my assumption. Wouldn't someone with whom you have a personal relationship work that much harder to keep you safe? I'll lay my bets on that one.

Dina returns. "I hope you all enjoyed some breakfast but it's time to take a little exam to help evaluate your thought processes and decision making abilities."

I whisper to my tablemates to build a little rapport, "Psych eval."

I get a few raised highbrows and a few nods. Vick also gives me a discreet thumbs up.

"So, if you could all please follow me, I'll lead you to the testing room. You can leave your trays."

We rise and follow her down the hall and enter a room more suited for voting. There are a dozen individual desks and each one has a cardboard blinder surrounding three sides, about twelve inches tall, just big enough that most people would have to partially stand to see inside another desk space, but short enough to see over casually. On each desk is a sealed test and a sharpened pencil. We file in. I sit down at a desk on the far right.

Standing behind a table at the back of the room is a tiny

Asian woman, about my height or maybe a tad shorter, very tiger-mom serious. We all look at her as we enter but she's giving off such a 'fuck you' vibe, no one actually makes full eye contact.

Dina does not follow us into room, disappearing after shutting the door behind us.

This whole ordeal is suddenly quite real.

"Please do not open the packets until told to do so," the woman says with a perfect staccato English, no accent whatsoever. I'm confident everyone in this room was expecting one.

"I am Dean Li Xia. I am in charge of the academy and will be administering the evaluation today. Underneath your test packet is a series of documents labeled NDA. Please take a moment to read through those pages carefully, then sign and date the final page. That bundle is your non-disclosure agreement. Take it seriously, as we take the privacy of this organization very seriously. I won't mince words. If you violate that agreement, it may result in your death. Take your time. After signing it, bring it to me."

This is kind of cool yet scary as hell. I've never seen a real NDA before. As I read through the legal jargon, I'm filled with dread. We're here for an orientation yet we've already been threatened with death.

There's a lot of talk about not revealing location specifics, organizational details and secrets, blah, blah, blah. I don't look too closely. If we don't sign, we can't stay. I'm way too curious to walk away now. I sign and date the final page as requested and give the packet to the Dean.

Once everyone has signed, the Dean goes on. "You will have ninety minutes, precisely, to finish. There are no right or wrong answers on this evaluation. Please use your best judgement and answer each one as honestly as you can. If you attempt to respond to each question with what you perceive to be a right answer or the answer you believe we would want to hear, you will be doing yourself a disservice. This evaluation is about you, not us. It is better to leave a question at the end unanswered than to pick a random answer. Any questions?"

I'm not sure the Dean took a breath while saying all that. No one raises a hand or speaks up.

"Good. Open your packets and turn to the first page. Read the instructions carefully. The timer starts in five ... four ... three ... two ... one ... begin." She takes a seat and starts using her phone, all the while keeping a close eye on us.

I tear open the round white sticker holding the packet closed and dive right in.

I fill in the space for my name and birthdate. The instructions are simplistic enough and basically reiterate what the Dean has just told us. Essentially, the evaluation gives you a two or three paragraph scenario and then three, four, or five responses to choose from.

For example, this is question four in my evaluation:

4.    Your name is Pluto PointBlank. You've been contracted to assassinate Mikey Mouseney, the head of a global conglomerate, mostly because of his involvement in a worldwide, underage, sex trafficking scheme that goes back some fifty years, and the powers that be have had no luck in prosecuting him for his crimes against humanity.

Just before you are about to complete your mission, Arnold Duckworth, a former high-level employee of the global conglomerate, gives you information that proves Mikey is innocent of this alleged wrongdoing, and that he himself is the responsible party. Somehow, Arnold found out what you were doing and is now trying to convince you that with new evidence, a different decision should be made.

You contact the organization you work for and share this new information; however, you have been instructed to proceed with the original contract and kill Arnold as well because he essentially caught you in the act and there can be no witnesses.

Which option will you choose?

A)    Do as instructed and kill both men.

B)    Kill only Mikey and threaten Arnold

C)    Kill only Arnold and leave Mikey alone

D)    Kill no one so that more information can be gathered


Yeah, this is some seriously weird shit. To me, there is an obvious answer, one that would please the Kill Academy. There is another answer, the one I would pursue if it were left up to me, but in this scenario, would not be correct. And yes, I know, the Dean specifically said not to go after the answer we think the company would want to hear, but that's total bullshit. One answer, A, gets you a job as a contract killer with an organization that can only exist when there is dogmatic obedience and predictability. The rest of the answers get you shipped home, period.

Ninety minutes roll by quickly. I doubt anyone actually completed the test. There were so many questions to answer, we could have been here for hours and never finished. I'm not sure they really need more than a few of these questions to get the psych analysis required.

"Put down your pencils and close your packets immediately," Dean Li Xia says. One of the male Tech Ops recruits ignores the Dean and tries to finish the question he is working on. The Dean is not pleased. With a raised voice, she says, "You're not going to do well here if you can't follow simple instructions." The man looks up and makes eye contact with her. "DO NOT piss me off." She pauses for a second and brings back a much calmer voice, serious and unnerving. "I'll claw your eyes out."

Even the biggest dude in the room is taken aback by her words, or more the tone behind them. Not one of us doubts she could rip any one of us apart. She may be the nicest person in the world if you know her, but to the uninitiated, she's scary.

Terrified and eyes wide, the man complies and pushes away a bit from his desk so it is obvious. He's battling whether to cry or throw up. Thankfully, he holds back on all counts.

The Dean jumps from her chair and quickly scoots from desk to desk collecting our evaluations and the pencils. She returns to the front of the class.

The only other woman taking the evaluation turns to me and softly says, "I need to pee, bad, like two cups of coffee bad."

I can see she's sweating bullets at this point and too afraid to ask Dean Sunshine. "Just ask where the bathroom is."

She shakes her vigorously and gives me a stern look.

"I need to pee," I blurt out, my head down and angled away from the Dean to throw my voice.

"Please return to the cafeteria. Enjoy a beverage. Someone will be around shortly to give you a tour of the facilities. The bathrooms are down the hallway where you woke up. Follow the signs." The Dean's tone is pleasant now, a complete one-eighty. Hot and cold this one is. Won't have any trouble judging her mood going forward. Yeah right.

I turn back to the woman. "Chicken shit. I'm Josey by the way."

"Emily. Thanks. She's terrifying."

"Don't let her scare ya. I'm sure she's more like a big fluffy kitten on the inside."

"Even kittens have claws."

I nod. My experiences at the animal shelter can attest to that. One kitten, no problem. Ten of them jumping all over you, that's another issue. Forty tiny little scratches on your hands and arms hurts like a son of a bitch.

"I could pee. Walk with me to the bathroom?"

"Okay," Emily says.

We jump ahead of everyone else and leave the room, heading down the hall toward the bathroom. A few of the guys eventually follow but most of them head straight to the cafeteria.

We find the ladies restroom and enter. As we use the facilities, we converse. I get right into the personal stuff.

"So, what the hell brings you to a place like this, Emily?"

"Oh, I don't know. I have poor decision making skills, I

think."

"I hear ya on that. They were watching me for a while. I guess they figured I could handle myself. I've never, you know, taken anyone out though."

"Well, obviously, I'm not here for that part of it. Truth be told, I kind of got caught on this itty-bitty credit card thing. Stupid mistake on my part. A very well dressed lawyer pops in, springs me, ends up offering me a chance to tryout here. I figured what the hell. Better than being in jail."

"Doesn't bother you knowing what this place is all about?"

"A little, but as long as I don't have to pull the trigger. If it bothers you, what are doing here?"

I ponder how to answer. It's not like I'm going to spill my entire life story to this chick, however, she's been rather forthcoming to me. I suppose I owe her a nibble.

"I'm not exactly an upstanding citizen myself. I can see some merit in what this organization does even though I may not agree with their motives. Hell, my life has been kind of a cluster-fuck lately anyway, bouncing from place to place. I figure it wouldn't hurt just to get the tour."

We exit our stalls at nearly the same time, wash our hands, walk out, and start heading back.

"Wouldn't hurt to have a friend around here, assuming we both make it," I say. "Not a lot of women in the ranks."

"Definitely. Thanks for the chat. I feel better about it now. You seem pretty cool."

"Thanks. You too. And good luck. We may not see each other once they break us up into groups."

"Same to you."

When we arrive at the cafeteria, the two groups have reassembled at their own tables, so we join our respective ones.

I pass on the idea of another coffee. My stomach feels uneasy in a way I can't pinpoint. I decide to sit next to a guy I hadn't spoken to yet. Don't even remember hearing his name during the introductions.

Before I can even pull the chair out to sit, this guy turns

his entire body toward me and gives me a stupid grin.

"Your periods synched up already?"

"Excuse me?"

"You deaf?"

"Settle down, Caleb," Vick says.

Ohhh, motherfucker. I need to put the hammer down on this asshole right now.

I grab a plastic fork off the table and kick the back leg of his chair to spin his body toward me. I then use the same foot to plant my boot firmly against his crotch and thrust the fork right to his face, jabbing into the skin right next to his left eye but not actually piercing. If he makes a sudden move, I can shish kabob his eyeball in less than a second.

"Listen, dickhead, the next time I hear you use my womanhood in even a remotely derogatory way, I'll pluck your fuckin' eye out and shove it up your ass. Capisce?"

The room is silent, everyone motionless.

"Well, Caleb? You get me?"

He gives me a soft nod.

"I see you're all making fast friends," Dina says from the doorway to the hall.

I remove the fork from Caleb's face and stuff it into my back pocket, slowing moving my foot away from his crotch. Caleb turns his chair back and looks away.

"Just demonstrating some ... techniques," Caleb says.

His snap response and cover bodes well for him with me. Honor amongst assassins. Not the total a-hole I figured. Still needs work with his sexist bullshit.

Dina sees right through it. "In any case, it's time for your guided tour." She steps aside. A tall, skinny ginger takes a step forward from behind her. He's as pale as Casper.

"I'm Marty. If the Tech Ops group will follow me, I'll be your tour guide for the rest of the day." He has an accent, almost southern but not quite. Maybe Midwest Southern.

The five of them leave their table and follow Marty out. Emily and I exchange a smile. I hope to see her again. I'm not sure why this surprises me but it's genuine.

"Okay, if the rest of you want to follow me, I'll give you the dime tour of the facilities and take you to meet some of the instructors," Dina says.

The group follows her down the hall to the right. I end up at the front of the pack as all the guys usher me forward despite my opposition. I prefer not to have people at my back, although, I understand the male-female social dynamic. Common courtesy, however, should always run both ways. I can imagine how funny we appear walking down the hallway - a giant pack of soldier boy brutes being led by a tiny, bitchy woman of ill repute.

We arrive at an elevator. Dina presses the down arrow, the door opens, and we enter. I don't know what the others are thinking but I sure as hell want to know exactly where we are.

"Where is this place?"

"The exact location is a secret. The sensitive nature of this organization demands it. In due time, some of you might be shown." Dina presses on button on the elevator panel labeled B2. "We're going to start at the bottom and work our way up."

When the elevator stops and the doors open, a short corridor of concrete and bright lights opens to a large room divided into two sections. The immediate left and right areas are carpeted and have expensive office furniture much like a doctor's waiting room except elite like an Ethan Allen showroom. The back of the room is twenty times the size of the waiting area and is closed off by a wall of glass with an oversized sliding glass door in the middle. Just above the door are a red light and a green light. The green is lit.

A middle-aged white guy is sitting to the left, his face in a magazine. When he sees us enter, he places the magazine on a nearby table, gets up, and walks toward us.

"I'd like to introduce you to Greg Mintz," Dina says. "He's our resident firearms and weapons expert. I'll just wait here and let him take you around this area and talk to you a bit. Greg."

Greg is thick. Neck like a linebacker. A person could

probably outrun him but if he ever got his mitts around your throat he'd have no trouble snapping you in half. He has a tat on each forearm. The left I can't decipher. It might be Greek or Latin, a short phrase. The right has an anchor and rope, an eagle atop it. Navy.

"Alright, listen up recruits. I'm Greg. You know that already. Should you join us here, this will be one of the first and most important disciplines you'll take on. If you intend to take out a target from distance, you'll have to be more than just proficient in firearms, you'll have to be sniper good. Most of that training will be done here in what we call The Cage." Greg waves an arm toward the giant room behind the glass. "This place is very sophisticated. We have computer controlled wind, light, noise, you name it. Eventually, of course, there will be more long range practice done at our outdoor facility, but that will come later. Any questions?"

"So, sniper rifles, but what about other arms?" Vick asks.

"We'll cover all the bases necessary for this kind of work. By the time we're done with you, you'll be able to handle a pistol, a rifle, a syringe, or the Vulcan neck pinch as well as you can handle your own cocks."

A couple of the guys glance over at me to catch my reaction to Greg's words. I don't respond. Greg makes no consideration for me as a woman on the cock joke, and that's a good thing as far as I'm concerned. I don't want exceptions to be made for me. As soon as someone starts seeing me as different or needing special treatment, their ability to train and teach me will be hindered.

"Follow me," Greg says, waving us on.

He steps to the glass door and it slides open automatically with a whoosh.

The group enters the massive room. On the right, there are a variety of shooting booths, a few concrete walls about two feet tall, a freestanding six-foot-wide wall with a window, and an eight-foot L-shaped brick wall. On the left, there are dummies made of ballistics gel in varying shapes and sizes, paper targets on wires, and a few sand barriers. Running all along the floor behind the items on the left is what looks like a giant stretch of treadmill belt.

"Go ahead," Greg says. "Get yourself familiar with the area. You'll be spending a lot of your time for the next several months in here."

We recruits meander about, separately, checking lines of sight, distances, and vantage points. I look to the ceiling and outer walls and discover what looks like giant fans cleverly hidden behind black mesh screens, the fan blades only visible up close. I'm a little worried about this part of the training but I hide my anxiety. Guns have never been my thing but they're going to have to be if I want to succeed here. One day at time.

"When it comes to advanced weaponry, you'll have access here to stuff that people don't even know exists," Greg continues as we step from place to place. "That's a real advantage in this line of work. Having the right tools can make all the difference. Of course, no matter how good the weapons, practice is the only thing that will make you great at using them. By the time I'm done with you, you'll either be a marksman or you'll be at home playing Call of Duty."

A few minutes pass and we gather near the entrance. I see Dina on the other side of the glass, standing ready to take us to our next destination.

"Any questions?" Greg asks. No one speaks up. "Don't worry, we'll have plenty of time for details. Hopefully, I'll see some of you very soon." He steps aside and ushers the group to the exit, and we leave him behind.

Dina awaits us. "What do you think?" she asks.

We all nod in approval.

"Pretty damn cool," Marcus says.

"This place is all kinds of crazy," Arnoux adds. "Never seen anything like it."

"Well, don't get too lost in the majesty of it all. This place is serious business. It will command your full attention." Dina looks to her wristwatch. "Time for Benjamin Nazar. He goes by Nazar here. He's our recon and stealth specialist. With him, you'll learn how to get in and out of places undetected. Not all missions allow for sniper shots from two thousand feet away."

She leads us back to the elevator, up to B1, and out to a similar setup as the floor below, except the corridor does not lead to a fancy waiting room. Instead, at the end of a short hallway there is a forty-inch-wide steel door with badge-only entry. A man, slightly shorter than Vick and perhaps of middle-eastern descent with black short-cropped hair is standing to the left of that steel door. His khaki colored t-shirt and cargo pants suggest he may have just gotten off a plane that originated in some war-torn desert country. Maybe he just likes the attire. Maybe he's just stuck in the past.

"Recruits, let me introduce you to Nazar," Dina says. "This is Josey, Vick, Caleb, Marcus, and Arnoux."

Nazar steps forward and gives me a nod with barely any eye contact. Nervous around women? He moves down the line and shakes the hands of the four guys, fully engaging them. Now I'm annoyed.

"Unfortunately, we can't enter the area right now," Nazar says. "It's under a massive renovation that's close to being finished but it'll be done by the time training begins next week."

"So, what's it like in there?" I ask.

"Better just to let you see it for yourselves, when it's done," Nazar says, still choosing not to look directly at me. "All I'll say is this, it's a big improvement over the previous area and much more realistic. It will serve you all very well."

I'm just going to keep myself front and center, hopefully force him to acknowledge me. "So, what's your story, Benjamin?" I add a little sauce to his name, just so he knows his ass is on notice with me.

Dina bails him out. "We'll save the more personal stuff for once you join the academy. Nazar is well-qualified and a valuable asset to the organization."

I lock my gaze on Nazar but he does not reciprocate, nor does he show the slightest sign of awkwardness. Tough guy.

I'll have my hands full with him. That's okay. I don't expect everything here to come easy.

"Thanks, Nazar," Dina says. She turns to us. "Okay guys. We're going to let you take a break and relax a bit in the food court. While you're in there, you'll be called one at a time to discuss your evaluation results with the Dean and myself."

We follow Dina back to the elevator as she goes on. "After that, we'll get a quick look at the Tech Ops side of the organization before a brief medical exam and fitting, then we'll get you outta here."

I expect to see the Tech Ops people at a table in the cafeteria when we arrive but they are absent. I decide to ask.

"Hey, Dina, will the others be joining us?"

"Nope. They've already left the building." She leans in close to me and whispers. "In case you're wondering, Emily made the cut. She'll be here next week."

"Oh. Okay." I feign indifference, taking a seat at the table our group had been at before. The fellas join me.

"I'll be back shortly. Enjoy some food and beverage if you need to." Dina hurries off.

"I'm just going to say what everyone else is thinking," Arnoux says. "This place is fuckin' awesome."

Vick chuckles. "You are a strange one."

"He's right though," Caleb says. "I've never seen anything like this before in my life. State of the art."

"You don't seem impressed, Josey," Vick says.

My mind is elsewhere. The true implications of this place are weighing heavy on me for some reason. If I join, my life formerly known as Josey 1.0 will be over and my upgrade will begin. I just wonder if I need this change. I'm on the verge of stepping over a threshold that cannot easily be undone.

"It's not that," I say. I decide to open up a little and see how these guys react. "It's just this whole ... killing thing. Doesn't bother you guys in the least?"

"Well, it's not like we're gonna be out there killing senior citizens and children," Vick says.

"You sure about that?" Caleb asks. "There's some rotten little kids out there."

"Aside from that occasional Damien from The Omen type kid, I'm sure the kill list is chock full of more true-to-life demon-esque motherfuckers," Marcus says. "These high price contracts aren't the kind reserved for taking out somebody's annoying neighbor. Right?"

"I guess so," I say. "But I guarantee you that sometimes a contract is not about good versus evil but more like killing in the name of convenience. You guys know exactly the kind I'm talking about here."

"You're right, Josey," Vick replies. "But let's get real for a second. We're all here because we've clearly demonstrated some level of ethical elasticity."

"That's a real nice way of putting it, Vick." I'm sure my face says it all.

"Oh, and you're the one person here that's a fuckin' saint?" Vicks says. "I call bullshit. There's no way you'd ever have even shown up on this organization's radar if you weren't involved in some bad shit. Don't you dare put yourself on some imaginary pedestal."

It's good to see Vick worked up a little. Let's me know he's not all skin and muscle and bone. He may even have a heart in there somewhere. Noted.

"I'm no saint, but what this company does, what we'll do, can't be compared to the petty shit I've been in. Bad behavior is certainly not black and white. There are degrees. I once stole and ate a strawberry from a grocery when I was ten. How much did that hurt the owners of the store? Probably not much, if at all. I take a contract to kill some CEO. Who gets hurt by that? Many. I just put an end to someone's life, possibly a son, a husband, a father. I also have to live with that for the rest of my life, which I would fully expect to be short in this line of work. There are ripples from this. What I've done, the things I tend to get into, don't even play in the same game as this."

"She's right, Vick," Arnoux says. "We can all forgive a fruit thief, but that behavior is not comparable to this. It's just not that simple."

"All right, all right," Vick concedes, putting his hands up. "I get it. You guys are right. We've been told this organization is quite discriminating when it comes to the kind of contracts it will accept. I'm choosing to trust in that. If you can't do that, you might as well leave now."

I have a hard time with trust, not something I give easily, and with the questionable means by which this organization got me through the door, I have no reason at all to just believe what they say about anything. My skepticism will remain. I don't think that means I can't be successful here. It just means I have faith in myself and will watch my ass, as I always have.

Our intense discussion is interrupted by Dina returning.

"Vick, you're up," Dina calls out from the doorway. Vick leaves with her.

Vick returns about ten minutes later, Caleb goes next, then Arnoux, then it's my turn.

Dina and I say nothing until we are sitting with the Dean in her office. The Dean has a single piece of paper in her hands.

"You scored well," the Dean says.

"Okay," I say.

"I also think you're full of crap."

"Tell me how you really feel."

"But you're smart, and we know you can see through this test." The Dean speaks calmly and directly. "That's part of the test, of course. You either answered every question in exactly the way you thought we would want you to, or you genuinely think this way. Which one is it?"

I shrug my shoulders and give her a sly smile.

"That's not really for you to tell us anyway, it's for us to determine. That's part of our responsibility. There is some disagreement here about whether you have the constitution for this work. I, for one, think you'll be a headache. Dina believes you could be great.

"So, I have one question for you, and the answer will determine whether you go back to the cafeteria or you leave here right now and never come back."

I swallow hard in anticipation. Does it really come down to this? I guess I'm about to find out.

"Why are you here?" the Dean asks.

How does one answer that?

"Answer quickly," the Dean snaps. "Give me your gut instinct."

"I need to think about that."

"No! I need the truth. Answer."

"I don't know."

"Yes, you do! Now say it!"

"I need a minute. Christ!"

"Josey, just say the first thing that comes to mind," Dina says, bringing some much-needed calm to the situation.

"Okay. Fine. Partially because I feel threatened, maybe because I want something more, but mostly, I think, because I'm curious."

"Good," the Dean says. "What are you curious about?"

"To see what this organization is all about."

"That's not really true, is it?" Dina questions.

I scratch the side of my head. "I guess I'm curious to see if I can do it. I honestly don't think I can, but I want to know."

The Dean gives Dina the slightest of nods, then they both rise from their chairs.

"You've passed the evaluation, Josey," Dina says with no emotion. "I'll walk you next door for the physical and a fitting for clothing."

I stand and we exit the office, leaving the Dean behind. I'm still a little worked up. I need a minute to myself.

"Can I use the bathroom?"

"Sure. You know the way. Go to this room when you're done," Dina says, pointing to a door with the letters MED on it. "Just return to the cafeteria when you're done with medical."

The bathroom is empty, as I was hoping. I lean on the counter, looking down to the sink, afraid for some reason to see the woman in the mirror. I wash my hands just to kill time. I admit I'm having some mixed emotions about being accepted. Can I pass the training? Yes, but the final step is actually pulling the trigger and I just don't know about that. Is there really any point in going through all this if when I get to the end, I freeze? Some of the people here think I can do it. Shouldn't that be enough? They're the experts after all, but then again, how can this kind of organization ever be trusted. Think about what they do for a moment. If they can perform that, it's easy to imagine that lesser evils wouldn't even register to them as such. I have to be careful here.

Something inside of me stirs. I finally bring my eyes to the mirror and what I see is a face screaming behind soundproof glass. I should run away but when I peer forward into my life, even just a few years, without this place I don't see anything. Either choice has risk. Both are dangerous ways to live. It's not like I'm going to go to community college and become a secretary or something. Can you imagine me typing memos and sending business emails, filling out TPS reports, collating and shit? That's hysterical. I am who I am, and that person has never been civil or nice. I belong in this world filled with monsters. Whether I like it or not, it goes down to the bone with me.

After getting my measurements for clothing taken and a basic physical, much like one might get before entering high school, I return to the cafeteria to find the guys sitting at the table, sipping on drinks and munching on snacks. Marcus is missing, in his meeting with the Dean and Dina.

"What's up boys? I see you're still here." I give them a devious little smile and sit down next to Vick.

"You ready for all this?" Vick asks me.

"You bet your ass," I answer more confidently than I actually feel.

Dina enters the room and comes straight to us.

"It's time for a quick tour of our Tech Ops area where you'll meet Marty and Tisha, the leads of our behind-the-scenes operational department."

We all head to the hallway together and Dina leads us to the right. We reach the only door at this end of the floor and are stopped by someone exiting that room.

From the doorway emerges a woman, maybe somewhere between fifty and sixty years old, dressed in a pinstriped pants suit, her jet-black hair in a bun. She's under six foot but tall for a woman, thin, almost lanky. She moves with authority, like with each step she fully expects people, hell, even the air in a room, to move out of her way. Our group unconsciously clears a path.

"Madame K," Dina greets with a nod.

"Dina," Madame K replies with a voice that is borderline majestic. For some reason, I expected her to have British accent, but alas, she's pure Americana, east coast. "I see you have our bright, young stars here. Please introduce us."

"Of course," Dina says then turns to us. "Group, let me introduce you to Madame K, she's the head of this entire organization." Dina turns back to Madame K and introduces us from left to right. "This is Caleb, Arnoux, Josey, and Vick."

There's no handshaking or anything, just nods and short hand waves from us.

She locks eyes on me. "Nice to finally put a face to the names," Madame K says. "I look forward to getting to know each of you as you progress." She stays on me and I'm starting to get uncomfortable. She finally breaks away and passes a glance and a smile around to all of us. "Don't let my title scare you. I'm here to facilitate your experience. We're a family and I want you to be comfortable. Just think of me as your life raft, ready to keep you afloat when you fall off the ship."

Compared to Dean Li Xia, this Madame K seems quite approachable. Good to know.

"When you're done here, Dina, would you please come up

to my office?"

"Of course."

Madame K walks off and heads to the elevator.

"Go ahead and enter," Dina says, ushering us through the doorway.

The first thing that comes to mind as I enter the Tech Ops area is the bridge of the Enterprise from Star Trek. Not that it looked anything like that but the room has a space-age feel, like a futuristic space shuttle. The room is shaped like a human eye turned sideways, the left and right walls curving away from the entry door and meeting up again on the other side of the room. Each of these curved walls is actually a giant computer monitor.

In the center of the room is a large computer console with Marty sitting on one side, Tisha on the other, facing each other. They have their own set of monitors as well, eight each, four on their lefts and four on their rights. The center of the console has an empty space, allowing them to view each other or the bigger wall monitors when needed.

The room is sterile, steel and aluminum, gray, but well lit. There is one exception to the sterility, however, and that's the tabletop surrounding Tisha. She's not exactly a neat freak. There are empty soda bottles, cupcake and candy bar wrappers, and a few paper coffee cups long past their usefulness. The only thing on Marty's side that suggests a human works there is a thermal mug.

When they see us, Marty and Tisha rise from their chairs and walk over to greet us.

"Hey guys and gal," Marty says with an outreached hand. "I'm Marty, this is Tisha. We run Tech Ops here. When you need help bypassing security, need a building blueprint, surveillance while on a mission, we are it. We can be your eyes and ears when you need them, so be nice to us." Marty shakes our hands and we offer up our names.

"Yes. These are two of the finest minds in the country when it comes to this stuff," Dina says. "They'll be a valuable asset to your missions, one you should never overlook."

"Yeah, so snacks and coffee are always welcome in here," Tisha says with a smile but she's serious.

"So, how long have you guys been working here?" I ask.

"I've been here for eleven years," Tisha answers. "He's been here ten. We know what we're doing, if you're concerned."

"Not concerned about your skill," I say. "Just curious what kind of shelf-life a person can have here."

"Josey? Jesus." Vick says.

"What? That's a legit concern."

"We do our best to take care of the people who work for us," Dina says.

"Of course, you guys aren't Tech Ops. More risk for you all," Marty says.

"Yes, yes," Dina intercedes, wanting to steer the conversation in a different direction. "We take the utmost precautions to ensure the safety of our entire force. Now let's finish up by heading back to the cafeteria. We need to discuss the protocol for your trips out of here and then back again on Monday, should you choose to continue on."

"What happened to Marcus?" I can't help myself.

"He will not be joining us," Dina says. "Follow me."

Vick gives me an elbow. We're all thinking it, I'm just the only one with the sac to ask.

Back in the cafeteria, we take a seat as Dina speaks.

"You've all been given a rare opportunity to do something special here. Whatever your reasons are for entertaining the idea, the time will soon arrive for you to make a choice. Will you join us to train, learn, and ultimately master the art of assassination, or will you go back to the lives you were living before you even knew we existed? Take the weekend to really ponder what this could mean for your life, your future. We sincerely hope you all accept."

I hadn't noticed before, but Dina is carrying a small canvas bag in her hand. She unzips the top and removes a handful of items. She lays a small stack of black business cards down on the table first.

"Each of you take a card. You must call the number on it by 6 pm on Sunday to share your decision. If you decide to come back, instructions will be given as to how you will return."

Vick takes a card and slides the others down the table. I take one and pass the others to Caleb and Arnoux.

"Now, each of you needs to take one of these pills." Dina twists open a bottle and shakes four out to her hand. She presents them to us and we each grab one. "These will not knock you out like the other ones but they will make your head spin a bit, make you a little silly. Go ahead, take them now."

We do so without question.

She tosses us each a black hood. "Don't put these on yet. I'm going to walk you out to a parking deck, and once you are in the SUVs, you'll wear the hoods and be taken home. Good luck to you all, no matter what you choose."

Vick stands up and shakes Dina's hand. "Thanks. It's been enlightening."

To be cordial, Caleb, Arnoux, and I follow Vick's lead and offer the same to Dina. With the official tour over, this will either be the last time I see these people and this place, or we're going to be students at the strangest academy I've ever heard of. My nerves right now are akin to a giant watermelon that just fell off the fruit truck. Good grief.

# 8

Saturday

Evie's going to shit a brick when she sees me with this pizza. I told her earlier in the week I would not be coming this Saturday and I've never shown up again so soon after a visit. And let me tell you, Giordano's Pizza is like catnip for little girl geniuses. She'll be borderline unhinged the whole evening, I guarantee it.

I had called Gabby and asked her if it was ok for me to stop by with dinner and hang out. She couldn't have been more thrilled. I told her not to tell the others though, I wanted to surprise them, especially Evie. It turns out, only she and Evie would be there anyway. Pete would be away for the whole weekend at a school math competition. The twins, Mandy and Randy, would be attending a friend's birthday party and not be home until late.

I'm going to be gone for several months. I have no idea what the future will bring for me. Just in case something happens to me, I have decided that tonight will be the night I tell Gabby the truth about her father. Of all the criminal behavior I've been wrapped up in, all the life-threatening situations, all the bold acts of physicality I have endured and dished out, the simple act of revealing a painful truth to people I care about will be the one thing that is my undoing.

My legs are heavy as I walk to their front door, my insides tight and uneasy, my breathing arduous. I just want to have a fun and relaxing evening hanging out with them, but at some point, I will have to veer off the road and plunge into the frozen lake that is my past mistakes. Before ringing the doorbell, I seriously contemplate just leaving and never coming back. I'm no quitter though. I won't leave. With the pizza in my left, I coerce my right hand to ring the bell.

I can hear the rapid footsteps of Evie running down the stairs and across the living room to the front door. A moment later, the door swings open and she appears, a smile so wide I assume her mouth and cheeks must hurt. All my worry melts away, for now.

"She told you, didn't she?"

She says nothing but somehow manages to smile even wider.

"Is that Giordano's?" Evie asks but she knows it is.

"Of course. Can I come in or you just gonna leave me outside all night?"

She franticly waves me in, then snatches the pizza and hustles to the dining room table with it. I follow, shutting the front door behind me.

At the top of her lungs she shouts, "Josey's here!" She turns to me. "I'll get some plates. You want water or pop?" She places the pizza on the end of the table.

"Water, thanks."

Evie sprints to the kitchen just as Gabby comes down the stairs.

I give her a look.

She knows I'm referring to the not-so-surprise surprise visit. She shrugs her shoulders and smiles.

I shake my head as she joins me at the table.

"Sorry. I told her she had to be home Saturday night and she would not stop pestering about why. I caved. Either way, we're happy you came."

"Me too."

Evie returns from the kitchen corralling three glasses of

water. After she places them on the table, she flies back into the kitchen without a word.

"Sit, please," Gabby says. She takes a chair to the left.

I go around and take one to the right.

"I admit, I was pretty surprised you wanted to come over so soon," Gabby says.

"Yeah." I say.

Evie is back from the kitchen with napkins and paper plates. She sits next to me.

I throw open the pizza box to reveal the extra-large pizza, half pepperoni and sausage, half cheese. We all dive in.

"Oh god, this is so good," Evie says between bites.

"So, what's this big thing you need to talk about?" Gabby asks.

Two big things, actually, but the one she is referring to is my Kill Academy training. I swallow and take a sip of water. "Well, I've had an interesting week, that's for sure. I just got a big job opportunity that sort of fell into my lap."

"Really? Nice," Gabby says.

"What kind of job?" Evie asks, mouth full of pizza.

"Will you please swallow before speaking?" Gabby commands. "Nobody wants your food spray all over the table."

"Sorry," Evie garbles, breaking the rule again. She covers her mouth. From behind her hand she says, "Sorry."

"That's the thing. I can't really talk about it."

Gabby gives me a funny look like she knows I'm up to no good. She isn't wrong.

"They are a very private kind of company and they don't really want me talking about it until after the training program." I know that's a lie, I'll never be able to talk about it, but it's the best I can do.

"Okay. That's a little weird. So, why did you have to come over with pizza just to tell us?" Gabby asks.

I can't get anything past her. "The training is a long process and could be three months or more. It's isolated and not around here, so I'll be gone for a while and won't be able to contact or see you guys for months. I wanted to tell you so you wouldn't think something was wrong if all of a sudden I seemingly dropped off the face of the Earth."

"Three months?" Evie asks. "Dang that's a long time. We can talk on the phone at least."

"Unfortunately, no. I will have no access to the outside world. It's crazy, I know. This company has ... trade secrets and they're very protective of them. It's a great opportunity for me."

Evie is frowning, while I can clearly see Gabby is deep in thought about all this. I know she has never fully trusted me. Why should she? She can tell I'm not always forthcoming. I have no discernible source of income yet I show up with bags of cash. I arrive in a different car every time I come to visit. I've never given her the full details of my relationship to her father. She has every reason in the world to be cynical. All the pieces, however, will fall into place for her tonight when I reveal the truth. Hopefully this will not be the final time I see the Leers. I would be devastated.

No one speaks for a minute. We continue eating. I dart my eyes around to gauge their body language.

"I wish you the best, Josey," Gabby finally breaks the silence. "We'll miss seeing you around here."

"Won't be forever." I think about the other thing I need to talk to her about and realize I may have spoken too soon on the idea of forever.

"Oh, this is too depressing," Evie declares as she pushes away from the table and rises from her chair. She storms off and into the living room.

"Evie," Gabby says. She looks back to me. "She'll be fine. She's infatuated with you."

"I know."

I swallow hard and take the opportunity to begin the other conversation I intended before arriving, words I've been practicing over and over in my head.

"Ya know, Gabby, there's something else I wanted to talk to you about."

"Oh?"

Before I can get another word out, the fierce, blaring sound of a house beat emerges from the living room. Gabby and I look to one another, confused.

Evie returns to the dining room.

"I don't want to be depressed, so we're gonna dance. Get up you two."

I look to Gabby again and we share a shrug.

"Come on guys," Evie begs. As the vocals start in, Evie starts whirling her hands in front of her and swinging her hips in time with the rhythm.

I can't help but smile and giggle.

Evie dances and hops her way back into the living room. We leave the table and follow her in.

We spend thirty minutes bouncing and stepping around the living room, shaking our booties to each new song – laughing, sweating, having fun - the kind I haven't had in a very long time. I'm normally quite reserved but I'm letting loose tonight. I need it. My life is about to get real strict. Hopefully, when I'm in the trenches of my new life, fighting for motivation, I can look back on this evening and remember what life is really all about.

We all drink some water to cool off and nibble the pepperoni off the last few pieces of pizza before returning to the living room to watch a movie. Evie insists on putting in the latest Pixar, which is great for me. Keep the mood light.

Halfway into the flick, Evie is fast asleep on the opposite end of the couch to me, her feet resting in my lap. Gabby is sitting to my right in a beige recliner that has seen better days. I look over to her and feel happy, then suddenly ashamed. Before arriving, I had fully committed to telling her the truth but now that the time has come to do so, I can sense the resolve leaking away like a small hole in my boat. Damn it.

I whisper, "Hey, Gab?"

"Yeah?"

"I need to tell you something, something about your father." I swallow hard.

"Like what?"

"On the night he died, I wasn't just there, I..." The words stutter from my mouth.

Gabby looks me right in the eyes.

I can barely stand to keep her gaze. I put my hand over my mouth. I weep, softly. Oh fuck. I can't do this. Tears begin streaming from my right eye.

"Josey, what the hell is going on? Why are you crying?"

"It was because of me," I choke out.

Gabby's face spells confusion.

I feel movement on the couch.

Evie sits up and rubs her eyes. "What's going on?"

Shit. I was only going to tell Gabby and let her decide how or if to tell the others. I can't do this. Not in front of Evie.

I turn my head.

Evie sees I'm crying and starts to get emotional herself, feeding off the negative energy that is permeating the room now.

I mouth the words I'M SORRY.

"God damn it, Josey! What are trying to say?" Gabby senses the truth of what I was about to tell her, something she may have known all along.

"I love you guys. I'm sorry. Please don't hate me." I shake my head. Through tears, I finally let the words go. "I'm the one that killed Wayne."

Gabby frowns, softly shakes her head. She tries to process the information but can't fully get her mind around it, I can tell. Her confusion spawns anger. With teary eyes, Gabby gets up from the chair. "Get the fuck outta my house!"

"There's a lot you don't know. I can explain. It was an accident."

Calm and firm, but seething with fury, Gabby says, "I want you to leave. Right now! And don't come back."

I can say nothing.

Evie is now crying much harder and totally at a loss about what has transpired.

What can I possibly say that will explain why I killed

Wayne? It was self-defense? He got caught up in some bad shit? It was either him or me? All of that is true but she won't hear the meaning behind those words, not in this moment. I guarantee all she can think right now is that her father is dead and the person responsible is standing right here - a liar, a murderer, an interloper.

"Please don't hate me. Maybe someday you'll let me explain." I turn to Evie. "Please don't hate me."

Fuck. I need to leave. I snatch my backpack off the ground and rush from the living room, out the door, and to my car. I don't even stop to process. I start the car, slam it into drive, and speed off to the docks.

I'm so pissed when I get home, I can't even sit down. I gather up the few personal items I have from around the boat, placing them into a few bags. I take a good hard look around the space. I'll miss the boat. It was isolated, quiet, and a good reminder of the positive affect I had on Janelle's life, but Monday I head off to the Kill Academy, and if all goes well, my days as a small-time hoodlum will be over.

I place my backpack over my shoulder, sit the two duffle bags and two plastic grocery store bags on the dock, and return to the boat. I left a red two-gallon container of gasoline on the boat a week ago knowing my time in this temporary domicile would be coming to an end soon. I grab the jug and open the cap, affixing the spout as I walk back inside the living quarters. Starting with the bathroom, I liberally splash the accelerant all around as I back my way out. I spin in a circle around the outer deck to douse that area as well before tossing the container through the doorway, back into the cabin.

I want nothing more than to stay and watch this fucking thing burn but I know I can't. I'll find a quiet place somewhere to park for the night and sleep in my car. I'll splurge a little tomorrow night and get a hotel room, maybe even get a massage and room service. I don't know that I deserve such fine treatment but my training isn't going to be a day at the carnival. I suspect I will be pushed harder than I have ever experienced in my entire life, even as challenging as my life has been. I just want a steak and a baked potato and some cheesecake. And a few pay-per-view movies. I know a guy at the Briarwood Hotel, a fancy five-star downtown that can get me a room without a credit card on file. Thom owes me a favor. About a year ago, I assisted him in fixing a money issue from a drug deal gone bad that he regretfully participated in. I haven't called the favor yet. This will be perfect.

I pull a matchbook from my front left pocket and walk to the bedroom. I strike a match and then set the entire book on fire. I toss the thing on the saturated bed and briskly walk out. Bags in hand, I jog down the docks and to my car. Once behind the wheel, I take a moment to look back at the boat and I can see a nice orange glow coming from inside the cabin. This was the one and only time I parked in the actual lot reserved for the docks, so I could see the marina perfectly. Time to get the hell out of here. Don't want to be anywhere near this area when that puppy blows. And it will. Once the flames hit the fuel tank – KABOOM!

Three blocks away, the sound of the explosion, even though I am fully expecting it, makes me jump. Another mile out, I pass a responding fire truck and police cruiser going in the direction of my handy work. I fight hard the temptation to stop and watch that son of bitch's boat burn but the wiser woman in me doesn't allow it.

I park my car about a half mile from the hotel, throwing most of my stuff in the trunk for safekeeping. I take a single bag with a change of clothes and my tablet. I throw the hood from my sweatshirt over my head and walk. I'm full of self-loathing. I hate myself for lying to the Leers but I think I hate myself even more for finally telling them the truth about Wayne. At least when I was the only one who knew the truth, the collateral damage was limited to my own psyche. Five people I care deeply about are now full of the shrapnel of my personal wars. I don't think I could look in a mirror right now without throwing up.

# 9

Day One
Monday

I arrived at the Academy in much the same way I did for the tour and psych evaluation - picked up, knocked out, dragged in. I wake up in a strange bed in a strange room. And with another headache. The windowless room is disorienting, no sense of time.

I get out of bed and start nosing around the room, just to get familiar with my surroundings. I discover quickly the answers to a few questions that have been bothering me. Considering how I was not allowed to bring a single item into the facility other than the clothes on my back, I wondered what I would wear while I'm here, and what I would do to entertain myself in my down time, assuming I got any. There's a hamper by the desk. I find a small laptop sitting on that desk, which when I open it reveals a boot-up screen unlike any I have ever seen, probably a custom Linux based system. I'll have to explore more of that later to see what I am allowed to do with it. Secondly, when I open the wardrobe in the corner, I find seven each of black tank undershirts, navy blue crewneck tees, black khakis, white cotton briefs, black mid-calf boot socks, white cotton quarter socks, and black sports bras. There are also two black zip-up hoodies. Resting on the floor next to the wardrobe are one pair of military grade black combat boots, a pair of black athletic shoes, and a turquoise pair of cheap flip-flops. I ponder the purpose of the dollar store sandals for a minute. Duh. Shower shoes. Safety first. If nothing else can be said, the organization is at least right on top of that deadly athlete's foot. Let's be real here. Itchy feet, itchy trigger finger. Am I right?

I wander back to the bed and note the time: 6:15 a.m. There is a utilitarian wristwatch next to the clock and a yellow post-it note on top of the alarm clock that I didn't notice before. It simply reads: Clean up, change into blues and blacks, athletic shoes, wristwatch, breakfast at seven.

I decide a nice, hot shower will be a great way to start the day, so I head down to the bathroom. I didn't see any toiletries in my room, so I go without. When I reach the bathroom, I see why those items were not around. On the counter, next to the sink, is a stack of towels and washcloths. Next to that a variety of hairstyling items – blow dryer, hair ties, bobby pins. I pop open the mirrored medicine cabinet and find bottles of lotion, foot powder, toothpaste, mouthwash, dental floss, packaged toothbrushes, bottles of aspirin and other anti-inflammatories, and cotton swabs. In the shower stalls, there are bottles of shampoo, conditioner, and body-wash.

I turn the nozzle of the shower to full hot and let it run for a couple of minutes while I get undressed. I use my shirt as a makeshift laundry bag, balling up the rest of my clothes into its center before gathering and tying it up.

I plunge head first into the falling spray. I'm trying hard to just relax and let go of my thoughts while I bathe, but the unknowns of this training have me on edge and brain-fried. Hopefully, the day will bring some solace. Being on the brink of something is almost always worse than the reality of it.

When I finish, I wrap a towel around my torso, blow dry my hair, and pin it back on the sides with a few of the provided bobby pins. I gaze at the woman in the mirror and wonder how she came to be here, where all this Academy shit will lead her, and whether she will ever see the Leer family again. I hope she gets a chance to explain and be forgiven. I know once I walk out of this room and put on the uniform, the woman in the mirror will be no more. I'll miss her, but evolution is inevitable.

I walk quickly back to my room to get dressed. The hall is empty. I wish the tech group's rooms were in this part of the facility too. I get why they isolate us at this point, but having a few other people around without all the pumped-up testosterone would be nice.

With no idea what we'll be doing today, I decide to wear a hoodie. If it happens to be chilly, I won't have to suffer all day.

Fast forward to after breakfast. The four of us – myself, Vick, Caleb, and Arnoux, ate and drank and barely said a word while doing so. The tension finally settled in, right down to the bone. Whether we are competing or not, the air filled with a pre-boxing match, fully focused Zen. We were all about the job, filtering the noise.

Now, we're all waiting in a part of the facility we have never seen. The door before us is gray painted steel and has a small square window. Vick peeks through and reports a small hallway, like a prison row, with five doors on the right, and a dead end. Inhospitable is the word Vick uses.

The Dean had led us down here, then promptly left, saying only that she'd return soon. So, we wait.

"Anybody in those rooms, ya think?" I ask.

"Maybe. Another test probably," Caleb says. "What you think, Vick?"

"Don't know," Vick answers. "We got a lot to learn. How much more can they test us without actually teaching us anything?"

Arnoux says his first piece of the day, "I got a bad feeling about this."

"You're paranoid," Caleb says. "Worried you're going to

be the next to go?"

The boys are playing mind games with one another already. I suspect they'll leave me out of it for the most part, me being a lady and all, but they'd do well not to underestimate me.

Arnoux smirks. "Bitch please. I can handle anything they throw my way."

"Yeah, we'll see," Caleb says.

"Yes, we will," Arnoux snaps back.

The two of them are almost in each other's faces.

"Settle down," Vick says. "This shit is gonna be hard enough without us fuckin' with each other."

"Vick's right guys," I jump in. "We're going to be pushed and pushed hard. No reason to put any extra sauce on it."

"Time to begin," Dean Li Xia announces from right behind us, scaring the crap out of all of us. We all look to her in amazement. Like a tiny ninja that one is. She could very well have been standing there the whole time. Damn she's good.

She moves past us, opens the door, and steps through. We follow her to the end of the hallway, to the last door. She reveals a key from her hand and uses it to unlock the cell door. She pulls it open, the metal scratching the concrete and filling the room with the most annoying grind I have heard in a long time.

"Caleb, this one is yours." She stands aside and Caleb enters.

"What are we doing?" Caleb asks.

"I'll explain in a moment," the Dean answers. She throws the door closed and locks it.

The remaining three of us pass glances and shrugging shoulders.

The Dean brushes us back a bit and quickly moves to the next and repeats, this time with Arnoux. The third goes to me, the fourth to Vick.

The inside of my cell is dank, all concrete except for the bucket in the corner. That damn bucket has me worried.

There is no bed, cot, or anything to sit or sleep on. The only light in the room is a faint blue glow coming through the tiny rectangle window in the door.

Loudly, but not screaming, Dean Li Xia says, "Endurance and isolation. That is your homework. That is your test. Plan to be in there for a while. If you don't go mad and you survive ... you pass."

Then silence. And more silence. After three minutes, we try talking to one another through the cell walls but the sounds from within are too muffled, so I sit.

First Three Hours: I sat against the wall and sang a few of my favorite songs from the 90s, recited my favorite poetry, pep talked myself into believing I've done the right thing by coming here. It would have been much easier if I had just gone to sleep, but it was still morning and I was still amped on coffee. Wasn't going to happen.

Four More Hours: I did a few jumping jacks, some sit-ups, but realized I should probably save my strength and energy. No telling when or if we'd get any food and water. I continued to pep talk some confidence in my decisions, not to mention that I definitely can't let Vick, Caleb, and Arnoux perform better than me. No way in hell.

Three More Hours: I could no longer hold my pee, so I put the bucket to use, air drying a bit before pulling my pants back up. I hoped to hell I didn't have an urgent number two to deal with. They didn't leave us any paper products. Dick move. I am thankful for the wristwatch with built-in LED backlight though, otherwise I would've had no idea it was about 6 p.m.

Two More Hours: Glad I wore the hoodie. As the sun went down, a chill settled in. I took off the hoodie, laid on my back, one shoulder touching the right-side wall, and used the hoodie like a blanket on my upper body. Luckily, the hoodie is on the longer side and works well. I hoped no bugs or rodents could get in the cell. I closed my eyes and tried to sleep. For the first time, I noticed my stomach rumbling with hunger.

I wake with a stiff neck and back. I do some stretching then check the time. 2:38 a.m. I'm surprised I slept that long but I'm happy about it. Time passes, mentally and physically.

# 10

Day Three
Wednesday

My third day at the Kill Academy is also our third day in confinement. I'd be lying if I didn't say this shit is getting difficult. Sleeping on this floor is messing up all my joints. My head won't stop throbbing either, presumably from the caffeine withdrawal, and maybe the hunger. Thankfully, my body has so far shut down the pooper. The smell of the urine is bad enough. I'm getting weaker by the hour. I wonder how the others are doing. They have a lot more body that can waste away than I do. I don't know how much more of this I can endure.

# 11

Day Five
Friday

I startle awake from that metal on concrete screech. I avert my eyes to allow for a light adjustment period. Two figures enter the room and stand before me.

One of them kneels down to me. "Josey, can you sit up?" Her voice is gentle, calming.

With all the strength I can muster, I use my arm to brace myself and push up, sitting against the wall.

"Good," the woman says. "I'm Jessica. This is Matt." She turns to Matt and is handed a small bottle of water and two pills. Back looking at me, she says, "Take these but go slow."

"What are they?"

"One is to help keep you from throwing up when you eat or drink anything for the next few hours. The other is a pain pill. I imagine your body is a bit wrecked from being on this hard floor?"

I nod, take the pills one at time with a little water, then chug the rest.

"Just sit for a moment. I need to check your vitals, okay?"

"Okay."

Both Jessica and Matt are wearing scrubs. Medical personnel for the organization, like the one that did our physicals during tour day. Matt hands her a blood pressure cuff and a stethoscope. She starts by measuring my blood pressure, then checks my heart.

They help me up and assist me out of the cell. A wheelchair awaits me in the hallway. They take me away and I'm left in my dorm with instructions to stay put, that food and drink would be brought to me, and that I would be assisted in the use of the bathroom and shower.

Being back in my room is better but I have a strong desire to go outside and see the sun. Hopefully, they'll let us indulge in a little fresh air. I wonder how the guys have managed.

# 12

Day Eight
Monday

They gave us two days to recoup after the isolation experiment. We rested and ate and were allowed to spend some time in a heavily secured outdoor courtyard. Unfortunately, Arnoux never left his room in that forty-eight-hour window. His body had failed him during the test, and even afterward, he was slow to recover. Late last night, four became three as they took Arnoux out of the building on a stretcher. I wouldn't have guessed he'd be the one to go down if it were assumed someone would. I figured maybe Caleb or myself. I hate that we had to endure something like that but I get it. It's taken me a couple of days of being out of the cell to acknowledge it. Just like with astronauts, on paper, a person can hit all the right buttons but until the real world, practical side can be applied and tested, an individual's ability to survive under certain conditions is unknown.

Today, we will engage in normal training, or so we've been told. The overall plan consists of three basic parts: weapons and firearms, stealth and penetration, and a broad-based strength, endurance, and hand-to-hand combat training. Our five days in the cell falls under strength and endurance. A trial by fire if there ever was one. The rest should be a walk in the park comparatively, and maybe that was the point of doing it right away.

Vick, Caleb, and I meet the Dean in the training gym on the floor below where our dorms, bathrooms, and dining hall are. Stepping out of the elevator, the hallway is the same L-shaped kind as the one above, with scattered doors, burgundy carpet, gray walls, fluorescent lighting. The door straight across from the elevator has a sign that reads: Fitness.

The space is much larger than I expect, well over two thousand square feet. Many of the walls are mirrored. There are televisions sporadically mounted on posts, all playing CNN, muted. Around the room there are groups of treadmills, ellipticals, weight machines, free weights, leg machines, and other contraptions I can't figure out how the human body can even fit in.

I can't fully describe how relieved I am to see this place. For some reason, I expected to have a six-foot long staff thrown on my shoulders with water-filled buckets on both ends. Then I imagined the Dean wiping my bare back as she guided me to the ten thousand mountainside stone steps that I would traverse every day for months on end. Ahhh ... treadmills.

We get no time to acclimate or chat after arriving. From behind us and out of nowhere, the Dean speaks. "Time to stretch."

We about jump out of our skins. I doubt we'll ever get used to her arrival. It's almost like she exists in the ether, manifesting instantly where and when she is required.

"Damn it woman! How do you do that?" Caleb asks.

"You want to learn?" she rebuts.

"Well, yeah," Caleb says.

Vick and I nod.

"Then don't ask stupid questions and do as I say."

"Yeah, stupid," Vick says, backhanding Caleb in the arm.

Somehow, the Dean is gone. Right before our eyes. We look to one another in confusion.

"Ahhhh!" Vick blurts in pain as his knees buckle, forcing

him to the floor. He moans with discomfort.

The Dean is right behind him. She had landed a blow to the back of his right knee. "When your target does not see it coming, that is when an attack is most effective. There is no better way to bring someone down than a force to the back of the knee, completely unawares." She floats around to be in front of us again. I brace myself as she passes, fully expecting to get dropped. I am spared, as is Caleb. She sure as hell has our attention now.

"Be silent and get up," the Dean commands of Vick.

He does but is clearly embarrassed. Not many people can get one over on Vick. He's one of those Best of the Best of the Best types. Never failed at anything in his life, top of his class, Boy Scout. Thinking about that for a second, I wonder how the hell he ended up here - where the outcasts gather, the ones who fell into the wrong crowds, or failed to meet some unknown potential. I'm going to have to dive into that one with Vick. There's clearly a story there and I'm dying to know.

"That is why I am the Dean and you are the students. You are stupid and weak and clumsy. But I will make you sleek. I will make you resilient. I will make you as light as the breeze."

We follow her to the back of the room to an open area for doing floor exercises. She has us sit on the ground and visually instructs us in proper stretching techniques, all the while giving us further details on what to expect for the many weeks to come.

"To get you in shape, you will be here every morning at seven sharp, except for Sunday, which is your day off. If you are even one minute late, I will whip your ass." We believe her. I plan to show up at 6:45.

"After that, you will clean up, have breakfast. On Monday, Wednesday, and Friday, Nazar will be working with you on your reconnaissance and penetration skills. If you can't plan a mission, can't get into places without being noticed, you won't last two days on the job. Those days with Nazar will be long. Fuel up. Sleep well.

"Tuesday and Thursday, Greg will have you. He will make sure the weapons of your choice become an extension of your very bodies. Let's remember the reason you are here, and that is to kill. Don't glamorize it. Don't try to fool yourself into seeing past the gruesome nature of it. You are here to learn to be a killer. Kill, kill, kill. That is what you are being trained to do, never forget it. Living the dark side of it is what will help make you great at it. Your motivations for being here are your own but the endgame is the same."

She lets the silence of the room settle in, looking to each of us to gauge our demeanor. We keep stretching and ask no questions.

"What you do on Saturdays will depend on your progress. You may get time for extra work in areas you are struggling with. Dina will likely meet with you on that day from time to time as well.

"Sundays, you rest.

"Successful trainees will be placed on three-person teams. One person is Point. They actually execute the kill. The Tech is responsible for surveillance, hacking, and research, though they work under the overall guidance of the Point. The third person is a Secondary Point. Should something go wrong and the Point can't complete the mission, the SP will step in and do the job.

"If you can't find success in any of these areas, you will go back to whatever life you were living before you arrived here. Plain and simple."

We end stretching as she finishes giving us the schedule. Following that, we get a lesson on how to breathe properly, calming our bodies, bringing our heart rate down. My body is starting to feel normal again by the time we hit the treadmill. After thirty minutes of light jogging, we do leg work on a few other machines, then she lets us off early. As the guys leave to get cleaned up, she pulls me aside.

"How are you feeling? The cell ... not an easy test."

I'm taken aback by her genuine concern. Until now, she has not exactly come off as the approachable type.

Straightforward, yes. No bullshit, yes. Relationship builder, I guess that's a maybe.

"Today has been a good day so far. That test took us by surprise, that's for sure."

She nods. "Can I offer some advice?"

"Absolutely."

"Don't get lost in your own story."

I give her a funny look.

"There is much to be gained by being here but don't let it define you. There is always more than meets the eye around here. Be who you need to be, do what you must, but never forget to see the bigger picture."

I ponder her cryptic words and wonder what lies behind the riddles. I can't help but let a bit of dread creep in. Her words are dire, sincere, and a warning, if I've ever heard one.

"I will. Thank you."

"Now go get cleaned up. You don't want to be late for your first day with Nazar."

I'm starting to get the impression there is more than meets the eye with the Dean. Her serious, no nonsense exterior may be just that – on the outside.

# 13

Day Seventeen
Wednesday

The morning workouts have been getting easier. I'm really starting to feel my legs under me as I run on the treadmill, not that concrete blocks for feet way I felt the first week, but more that confident Clydesdale kind of way. I'm feeling like a thoroughbred trotting down Main Street for the St. Patty's Day parade. I think I need a slow-motion jogging montage showing my feet completely off the ground as I glide along, my hair flowing in the breeze.

Now cleaned up, fed, and hydrated, I'm ready for session number five in stealth and recon. What sexist bullshit I briefly had to deal with from Caleb has been trumped by Nazar. Maybe I'm reading him wrong but he barely makes eye contact with me and never picks me to demonstrate anything. Maybe it's because he would prefer not to touch me for some reason, and I get the impression he has been giving me a free pass when it comes to evaluating my performance. I've thought about discussing it with the Dean or maybe just throwing my concern by Vick, but I don't want to be that person – the one who whines to the boss because their co-workers aren't being nice to them. I admit, I'm already pretty fucking good at this shit. I've done my fair share of B and E, lurking around in the shadows without being seen. This job, however, demands more and I don't want to take shortcuts. I need to find a way to break through the bullshit with Nazar.

Do I challenge him straight up, see how he reacts? Could be risky. I don't know how the organization will view such insubordination. Will they see it as strength or stubbornness? Deviance or duty? Maybe I can find a way to back him into a corner and force him to acknowledge me. I could purposefully fail at some test. Someone will see it. I know we're being watched. The organization is always watching, judging. Either way, I think today is the day.

I lead Caleb and Vick through the door to our recon area of the basement levels. We don't see Nazar but he could be hiding anywhere. The space is designed to look like a brick two-story building, complete with streets, an alley, a fire escape, and a flat rooftop. The height of the room is likely around fifty feet. When one enters the space, the first twenty-five feet is the street, two lanes wide with a few cars parked in scattered locations. At the moment, the space is fully lit, like high noon on a summer day. If we couldn't see the ceiling, we might not know we were actually indoors.

Before we can get ten steps in, the lighting of the entire area switches off for five seconds, then a few select lights turn back on, giving us a street and building like midnight. Most of the windows of the building are dark. There are a few streetlamps on and the red glow of an exit sign down the left alley is barely perceptible. The ceiling is now filled with tiny, softly flickering LEDs made up like the stars in the sky. Not too realistic but it doesn't need to be. We get the idea. How they illuminate is the point.

Still no sign of Nazar, then his voice emerges from some unknown point in the space.

"There are three items on the second floor of this building, in different locations. You will have no trouble entering the building without being seen, however, once inside, you must completely avoid detection by the staff working there."

The voice stops. We look at each other with varying degrees of interest. I wave the idea off like it'll be a piece of cake. Then again, if it's so easy and yet I fail, I might be able to expose Nazar's behavior towards me. Vick rubs his hands together, ready for the challenge. The voice from the beyond returns.

"In the backseat of the red sedan parked on the street, there is a file folder for each of you with a detailed briefing of the mission, building analysis, tech specs, everything you will need to succeed, save for your own execution skills. You must each retrieve one of the items and make it back to the street undetected. You may choose to assist one another, if you like, but it is not required, and ultimately, you are solely responsible for the retrieval of your assigned item. You have one hour. Begin!"

The guys rush to the red sedan to get the folders. I walk slowly toward them. Vick hands mine to me. I don't bother opening it. As Caleb and Vick read through theirs, I just stand still, staring at the cover, the initials J.B. written in black marker.

"We'd probably get through this quicker if we work together. One entry point, one path to the second floor, much less likely to be detected," Vick says.

"Agreed," Caleb says.

"I have no intention of doing this. Better if you guys just go on without me. I don't want to jeopardize your missions."

"Whatever, Josey," Caleb retorts. "Seriously, Vick's right. We'll get through this faster as a team."

Vick looks me right in the eyes and can see the truth of my words. "What the hell are you talking about," he says.

"I'll tell you guys about it later, assuming I'm still here after this."

"You're not making any sense," Vick says. "Whatever is bothering you, we can discuss it after the training. Now open your folder and let's get going."

"Not gonna happen. Now go on before you both flub this up. Time's a ticking."

"Damn it, Josey, you're being," Vick stops mid thought. "Fine. Caleb, let's hit the alley. There's a small window that leads into a storage room where no one is likely to be. Once in, we can discuss the rest of the plan." He jogs off to the alley.

"Perfect," Caleb says before turning to me. "You better get your shit together. Nazar is not going to like this."

"That's just it, Caleb. I don't think he'll give two shits."

"Your funeral," Caleb says as he shrugs his shoulders and runs off to join Vick, leaving me alone in the street.

I'm not really alone though, am I? I know Nazar is watching, listening. I'm sure the organization is too. I'm taking a big chance here but if I don't do something, we all lose. I just hope they'll see my act as one of simple protest. They might just kick me right to the fuckin' curb.

I walk over to the sedan and return the folder to the back seat. To end the charade quickly, I go straight to the front of the building, pull open the double doors in dramatic fashion, and strut through like a woman on a mission, although, not the mission they are expecting.

It dawns on me as I step in, my entrance might be the perfect distraction for Vick and Caleb to get where they're going, so I decide to make a loud scene.

Fully in the lobby, the lady behind the front desk sees me and isn't sure how to react. To draw the attention of everyone I can, I start to sing, quite loudly, my favorite song from when I was eight years old, "All the women who are independent, throw your hands up at me."

People gather from all over the first floor in response to my bellowing. I hope the guys realize what's happening and can take advantage of it. Their path upstairs should've just gotten much lighter.

As I hit the fourth line of my song, the receptionist shakes her head in disapproval, and I simultaneously feel a pinch in my neck. I reach around to swat at whatever hit me to discover a small dart hanging from the skin, just to the right of my spine. I pluck it out and bring it around to look at, but my vision is already blurring. The dart hits the floor four seconds before I do.

My eyelids flutter open to find Jessica, Madame K's assistant right in front of me, sitting behind her desk, typing away on her computer.

I quickly straighten up in my chair. The blood rushes to my forehead. I rub it, sigh, and close my eyes for a moment.

"I don't suppose I could get some water and a couple of aspirin?" I ask.

"Sure. Hang on." She rises and disappears down the hall for a minute. She returns with a small bottle of water, handing it to me before sitting down. She then pulls open the top left drawer of her desk, sifts through the contents, and finally produces a clear bottle of aspirin. She removes two pills and hands them to me.

I pop both into my mouth and gulp the entire bottle of water.

"So, what's going on?" I ask.

"Li Xia is in there right now with Madame K, I assume discussing you. This place is all abuzz about what you did. Ballsy. Stupid ... but ballsy."

"Ah. Glad to see I'm having such an impact."

From inside Madame K's office, we hear a raised voice but nothing coherent, and the thud of a hand slamming down on wood.

Jessica and I exchange a scared look.

"I guess you're going out with a bang."

"Shit."

The office door behind me flies open and the Dean emerges. She's walking briskly. The door slams shut, shaking the walls and the floors.

"Follow me, Josey," the Dean commands.

"Well then. Madame K is not pleased," I say.

"She slams that door like twenty times a day. I think it's a stress release for her," Jessica says.

"Does it work?"

"You're about to find out."

"Fair enough."

The Dean and I walk to her office where we take seats at her desk. She sits for a moment in silence, trying to find calm.

"Josey, Josey, Josey."

"That's my name, don't wear it out."

"What the hell were you thinking?" the Dean says, raising her voice slightly. She places her hands on the arms of her chair, her fingers tapping.

I'm not stupid enough to answer her clearly rhetorical question.

"We're all quite frustrated with you, Josey. Hopes were high. You're not leaving us a lot of choice here." Her tone and facial expression has changed from angry to that parental grand disappointment, a look of - I just don't know what to do with you anymore.

"Are you bouncing me? Don't you want to hear my side?"

"Oh, I have no doubt your actions have reasons. Maybe if someone were made aware of those reasons before you pulled a stunt like this, a solution to whatever perceived issue you have ... could have been found. You've made yourself look like a fool, and worse yet, made Nazar out to be one too."

"Well, Nazar is the problem. He won't even look at," the Dean's raised hand stops me.

"Have you ever had a conversation with Nazar, a real one? The answer is no. You're presuming to know something about a man you've barely spoken to."

"He doesn't exactly seem receptive to me. No eye contact, quick words and phrases. Yes, no, good work. Won't even touch me on the arm. What am I supposed to do with that?"

"I forget sometimes where you're from."

Her tone pisses me off. This street rat is about go street tiger. "Meaning?"

"This is a business, a corporation. You've never worked in that environment, clearly."

I had no idea she was going that direction. "Assholes here,

asshole there. People are people."

"Exactly my point. In your world, you butt heads with someone, you fight them or you disengage. In the real world, we must learn to coexist within large groups of people that have many personalities and idiosyncrasies. The entire business world collapses without learning how to do that. YOU," she points at me, "need to learn how to do that."

"Not really your concern now since you're kicking me out."

The Dean throws her head back and lets out an odd chuckle. "Oh, Josey. Madame K sure as hell wants me to throw your ass out of here but she's left it to my discretion. So, no, you're not going anywhere. Another thing you need to learn. If we threw everyone out of here for every little mistake they made, well, we wouldn't be sitting here talking. Do you know how many times I've had Amatto in here for some ridiculous crap he pulled during training? More than I can remember."

That's a relief, but there's still the issue of Nazar and his behavior towards me. I assume they're going to punish me somehow for this. God, I only hope I don't end up in the cell again. Not the cell, not the cell, not the cell.

"So, what now? I feel like I might be losing something while training with Nazar. I don't feel I'm getting a fair evaluation from him."

"I've noticed."

"Of course you have. I'm sure you guys see everything." That was snarky of me. I better reign it in. I don't want to push my luck. "So why hasn't something been done? Is my training not suffering because of this?"

"You really believe that? You could *teach* stealth and recon here. If I thought for one minute there was a real problem, I would have stepped in. You should've voiced your concern though. This is not the kind of business where we leave too much to chance. Our lives depend on it. For future reference, don't ever be afraid to come to me with real issues."

I try hard not to reveal how flattered I feel. Maybe she's

just buttering me up before putting the hammer down on me. It's funny. My first impressions of Madame K and the Dean are now reversing. I find that interesting yet somehow troubling. Boat raft my ass.

"I get it. I'll work harder on that going forward."

"You had better."

"So, if I may ask, what exactly is Nazar's problem with me? I thought it was just some misogynistic bullshit at first, but now I'm not sure."

"I applaud your personal crusade against the social injustice that is women's rights, however, Nazar is not your enemy in that battle. Without saying too much, let's just say, you remind him of his daughter Leza."

"Hmmm. Okay."

"She was a soldier in the Israeli army. She was killed during a peacekeeping mission about eighteen months ago. He cannot help but think of her when he sees you."

"Oh shit! I had no idea."

"Of course you didn't. How would you?"

I sigh. "What can I do?"

"That's up to you. If you like, you can try to have a conversation with him about it. Otherwise, let it be. Just know, I'm monitoring the situation and will make sure your training is not adversely affected."

"Okay."

"Now, go get something to eat. It's lunch time and I have things to do." She rises and waves me off with a flick of her fingers.

# 14

Day Nineteen
Friday

After morning workout, I see Nazar in the hallway on my way to shower. Against my better judgment, I decide to stop him for a chat. I know at some point I'll have to face him, might as well be now with no one else around. I do this under the assumption that the Dean has already spoken to him about my actions.

"Hey, Nazar, can I talk to you for a minute?"

"Yes. I need to speak to you as well."

"Let me just first apologize for my behavior. I should have tried to talk to you before pulling that crap. It was not very professional and it won't happen again."

"I know you spoke to Li Xia. She explained what happened, and it appears I should be the one apologizing. I let my personal issues affect my work and you may have been paying the price for that. I reciprocate your promise to not let it happen again. So, we're good here."

"Okay. Thanks. I have a great respect for you, and I just want to excel here. I don't think I can do that without your training."

"I appreciate you saying that, but I think we both know that's not entirely true. Some of my behavior has nothing to do with Leza. Some is because recon and stealth is one area you're miles ahead of the others. An idiot could see that from day one. Having said that, I'll make certain you are not shortchanged here. Where I think you need improvement, you'll hear about it, otherwise, I suggest you put your energy in Greg's training. Sound good?"

"Yes. Thanks again. I need to get cleaned up or I'm going to be late for your session. So, I'll see you in a bit."

Nazar nods and waves me on.

I head off to shower. That went better than I could've imagined. Phew. A weight has been lifted, that's for sure. Maybe I can concentrate now.

This whole incident was such a distraction for me. There's an interesting dynamic that exists around here. On one front, we are training to do a job that requires stealth, secrecy, deceit, and a certain amount of detachment. Yet, on the backend of this place, our training and job performance require honesty, frankness, and unity. Acclimating to the yin and yang nature of this business will not be easy, and may, in fact, end up being the most difficult mountain for me to climb.

# 15

Day Twenty-three
Tuesday

It only took me a few minutes of being around Caleb and Vick to figure them out, but our firearms instructor, Greg, has been a tougher nut to crack. I think I have him down now.

He's a great teacher and surprisingly patient, but he has his triggers. On the surface, he's obvious. Ex-military - so he's sharp, direct, keeps the food on his plate quarantined, team player, intense. He's been divorced three times and is currently single, probably for the best. No kids, also probably for the best. Can you imagine being the child of an overwrought disciplinarian with PTSD and unresolved anger issues? Jesus! That kid would end up a mess.

I sense, however, turmoil within the man, an elusive personal wrangling with some form of self-loathing. Maybe it's just the family thing, maybe he's seen one too many horrible things from his days in the military. I don't think those are what is eating at him. He comes off to me as a man who is holding a secret. Of course, my curiosity on the matter is driving me insane. But do I really want to pull the crazy curtain back on this guy's past? Probably not.

Our first two sessions with Greg on our ninth and

eleventh days here were fairly mundane but interesting nonetheless. Upon entering the shooting area, we discovered three long banquet style tables end-to-end, all with various weapons laid out down the entire length. We gathered at one end and Greg gave us a rundown of each weapon – their origins, their tactical advantages and disadvantages, variations that might exist for each one, and a cursory explanation of how to care for each weapon to keep it in prime condition.

I'm a blade girl, a stun-gunner, a woman with a big stick, and though I've used a gun, I would not call myself even slightly effective in their use. The table was filled with visually familiar items, but from a practical standpoint, most of the guns were foreign to me in terms of usage. This training will be the most critical for me, as I am a novice at best, and it's essential to the nature of this business. Picking up the first long-range rifle and learning to hold it correctly, Greg tapping my elbow to keep it high, my shoulder next to the butt, never directly behind it, left me anxious and with the only true sense of doubt in my own abilities since I had arrived.

We didn't fire any weapons on those first two days, just got the detailed overview. Vick and Caleb are intimately familiar with many types of guns, so their training will be easier. That's probably a good thing, as I'll need more attention from Greg to get me up to speed. And he promised to work with each of us at a pace and level we are comfortable with.

On our third day, Greg took each of us aside and got a more detailed picture of our own personal levels of expertise. He would hand us a weapon and ask us to tell him its make and model and any other pertinent information we could remember. Let's just say, Vick and Caleb did most of the answering, I did most of the shoulder shrugging.

We spent the rest of the day disassembling, cleaning, and reassembling many of the weapons. That was our first lesson in getting to know the firearms, inside and out. He also made us aware of the many types of ammo that could be used with each one, including tactical reasons for each. There was so much information I could barely keep up. Those first three sessions were the only times so far that this place truly felt like a school to me. On those first days, the only difference between this place and high school, at least for me, was instead of Bunsen burners and textbooks, we handled guns and ammo. And the obvious, of course, here, if you step out of line, the instructors might just kick your ass.

Day four of weapons training is here and we've been informed we will finally get to fire a gun.

"'Bout damn time," Caleb hollers. "Give me the biggest one you got."

"Son, you better settle your ass down," Greg commands. "You'll get whichever one I want you to have."

"Yes sir," Caleb says with a salute.

"I'd ask you kindly not to address me as sir. The next time, I'll ask you with my foot up your ass. Call me Greg, or Mr. Mantz if you absolutely must be a pretentious asshole."

Greg takes Vick and Caleb down to the end of the table. While getting them up and running with large, high-powered rifles for target practice, I run my finger along the edge of the table past each weapon, curious to know what Greg will do with me.

The boys have ear and eye protection on in a matter of minutes and are firing away. I hear Greg talk to them about how their accuracy will be assessed, weak spots determined, and more practice encouraged in places where the most improvement is needed. Greg tells us all we have to achieve a certain level of shooting accuracy with a wide variety of weapons before we graduate to something more akin to live targeting. He tries to be vague but hints around to something like each shot needing to be within three inches of a targeted area, ninety-plus percent of the time. This will be variable based on conditions, weapon style, target type, and so on.

Greg finally gets to me.

"Just so you know, I've only fired a few guns in my entire life, basically .9 millimeter types."

Greg rubs his hands together with joy. He seems excited for the opportunity to train someone from the ground up - a true pupil.

The first loaded gun he hands me is a single shot, .22 caliber beginner's rifle. We go over all the gun safety basics: Always point in a safe direction, don't put your finger on the trigger unless you intend to fire, and understand what and where you're shooting, among other things.

I put on the ear and eye protection, and fire fifteen times, hitting the target with fourteen. Only five or six of the shots would've killed the person, had the paper target actually been flesh and blood.

Greg presses the button to bring the target to us. "Not too bad, Josey, not too bad. And you never used a rifle like this before?"

"Nope. Shotgun, but ... you don't really need to aim well with one of those."

"Give me that."

I hand Greg the rifle. He walks it over to the table of guns and picks up another one and a box of ammo. He hands me the .45 caliber weapon. The heaviness surprises me. For a small gun, it has heft. I pop the clip and load the ammo.

In an effort to lighten the mood and have some fun, I carelessly point the gun down range, turn my wrist sideways like a fuckin' gangster, and fire just one shot. The unexpected power from the kickback wrenches my wrist, throwing the aim wildly off. No one knows where the shot lands. Luckily not in anyone's ass.

Embarrassed, I pop the safety on. Before I can fully turn to face Greg, he is already right next to me. He snatches the gun from my hand, checks the safety, and gives me a look of stern disappointment.

I mouth 'sorry' to him but he doesn't want my apology.

"Have fun with Nazar, have fun with the Dean, but in here, where a simple accident can kill someone," Greg says, then pauses. He shakes his head, slowly, in the most dramatic way a person can.

I get the message. I don't speak. I give him two quick nods.

He doesn't say another word to me, just points at the exit, marking the end of my firearms training today.

He's right, of course. Lesson learned.

# 16

Day Twenty-seven
Saturday

"So, how are you feeling, Josey?" Dina asks, a pen and notepad in her hands. She's sitting in one of the two brown leather club chairs in her office. I'm parked in the other one, just across from her. We've had a couple of these little psych meetings since training began but I don't offer much. I don't want them in my head any more than is absolutely necessary. I spend most of my time with Dina diverting, fake acquiescing, and studying the room.

The office is modern and clean but lacks personal items. One might expect to find her degrees framed on the wall, a picture of a husband and kids, but the only thing that looks like it might be personal is a small ivy houseplant in a fluorescent orange pot sitting atop her black, four-drawered filing cabinet. Why do I think the pot is personal? A decorator wouldn't pick that color for this office in a million years. It's wildly out of place. That pot means something to Dina. A gift from her daughter for Mother's Day? Everything around here is so impersonal and it makes sense to have it that way. This work is dangerous and it requires that kind of detachment. I'm intrigued though. Through the organization's own investigation of me, they could write my biography and

I'd very much like to level the playing field in some way.

"It's been an interesting few weeks. What's with the orange pot?" Diversion.

She looks over at the pot like she needs to be reminded it's there. "Caught my eye one day. How well do you think you're doing here?" Diversion countered. Game on. She's asked me that same exact question at every meeting.

I pretend I didn't hear her explanation for the pot. "Your kid get it for you or something? It's cute." I know she's way too good at this shit to fall victim to my badgering but what kind of patient would I be if I didn't play my part.

"Josey, we are here to talk about you, not me. Nice try though. Want to try again?"

I figured as much. Maybe someday I'll get her to slip up if I just keep at it, or so I keep telling myself. I respect her professional nature. If I had to choose anyone in this organization to get the scoop on, it'd be Madame K or Ollie, not Dina. Thinking about the skeletons that must be in their closets, I get all giddy. Then again, they might be more horrific than I would ever care to know about.

"You talk to Nazar?"

"You're really good at answering a question with a question," Dina says.

I give her only raised eyebrows.

"I speak often with Nazar. About what are you referring, specifically?"

"Oh, ya know ... The Incident."

"You sure know how to make an impact. Yes, yes. All of the leadership here have spoken in depth about your actions, and the hows and whys of them. It's been what, a week now. Certainly, you know conversations have been had?"

"Sure. I just wanted to see if you'd be honest about it."

"Fair enough."

"Training is going well. Nazar and I cleared the air. I'm improving with the weapons training. Not much else to say."

"You seem tired. Are you sleeping enough?" Dina asks as she makes a quick scribble in her notebook.

"We've been pushed pretty hard. A little cabin fever. Be nice to see the water, a busy street corner, anything, quite frankly, that isn't this gray fuckin' place."

"Would it help to know we have a little field trip planned for very soon?"

"Now you're speaking my language. What's the trip?"

"Can't say just yet but you'll enjoy it."

"It could be an insurance seminar or a root canal, if it's out of this building and I get to see the sky, I'll be happy."

"It'll be mostly outdoors and that's all I can say."

"Nice."

"Anything you need to discuss?"

I give her a queer look. "Yeah, like all the other times I've been in here."

"I do hope your withholding is not because you don't trust me. Is that the case? Because in a place like this, having an outlet is critical."

"I understand. Truthfully, I do trust you. At least as much I can trust anyone here."

"I realize this environment doesn't easily breed trust but if you expect to last, you'll have to find a balance."

I nod with all sincerity.

"If you don't have anything to add, I guess we're done for today," Dina says.

"I do have one ... kinda weird question."

"Please."

"What is the organization's take on internal fraternizing?"

Dina tilts her head and purses her lips trying to determine my meaning. "I assume you mean romantic relationships amongst the recruits?"

"Something like that." In truth, I wasn't really interested in acting on such desires, and it wouldn't be with a fellow recruit anyway. I just want to know the kind of protocol breech I might get into if something were to happen.

"There is no rule in place, however, step lightly in that arena. This life is complicated enough without internal romantic entanglements. Once your training is complete, there will be a franker discussion about that with the team when it's set up."

"We've been told a little about this team. Care to share more about how that works?"

"I can't reveal any more than that until training is complete. Sorry."

"You're a big tease, you know that?"

"All in good time, Josey. All in good time."

"I didn't really have anything else, so, are we done here?"

"Yes. Thank you for coming in."

"A painful pleasure, as always," I say. "Have a wonderful day," I sass.

Dina closes her notebook, places it on the desk with the pen, and picks up her office phone. "See you next time."

# 17

Day Thirty-seven
Tuesday

Seeing the sky for the first time in just over a month, even though it's cloudy today, is making it hard to concentrate on the training. Greg knew it might be a problem. He briefed us on the phenomenon. "All recruits get a little stir-crazy," Greg said. "The first time out of the building can get overwhelming and it can be hard to focus. Just try to remember why you're out there. It won't be the last time you go out, only the first of quite a few excursions."

I heard his words. I let them settle in. But that sky. That fresh air. Ahhh. That damn sky.

Going forward, we've been told we will no longer need to be drugged when we leave the facility, which is a relief. Damn pills they give to knock us out make for an awful headache. There's still some secrecy involved. They plug our ears, cover our eyes, and bag our heads, but that's a far cry from the alternative. And then there's the driving around for hours before arriving. No sense of true distance. Home base could be anywhere. We recruits have a running bet as to what large city we are closest to. My money is on the New York Metro.

I'm kneeling behind a barricade made of sandbags. Ten feet away on my right is Vick, Caleb on my left. We're in a lightly treed area, remote. There is a clearing just ahead of us, nestled perfectly into the surrounding brush. I feel more like a soldier out here than an assassin. Granted, I'm used to a more urban setting, but my new position might require me to work in any number of different locales. I suppose the stereotype of the lone gunman up on the twentieth floor aiming at a target in a building just across the way might be just that – an overplayed movie stereotype. I can well imagine knifing someone in the back, poisoning a drink, blowing up a vehicle. The long-range rifle shot is probably the easiest to pull off in most cases, but some clients will prefer means other than firearms for any number of reasons. That is why our training has been so diverse. Today, however, is all about that sniper rifle - my weakest.

My elbows rest on the sandbag, my left hand holding the rifle steady. I don't like the larger ear covers, so I choose to wear ear inserts. My eye protection is standard issue. Greg is right behind me, watching and waiting. I've missed a few shots today, been slightly off target on many others.

I place my right hand firmly on the back end of the receiver, my index finger rests parallel to the trigger. I peer into the scope and locate the target, some one hundred yards away. I take my eye away from the scope and twirl my neck to stretch and release some tension. I see the sky again and my gaze lingers.

"You okay there, Josey?" Greg asks.

Oops. Lingered too long.

"Everything is great. Staying loose."

"You bullshitting me?"

I put my eye back to the scope and assume the proper position again. "No sir."

"I told you not to call me that. My father is a sir."

I raise my right hand and give him the OK sign.

Somehow, I can hear the doubt on his face. For now, he lets me be, moving on to Caleb.

I see the target again - a life-size paper version of a man's head and torso. I desperately need to put a few right through the heart and eyes of my two-dimensional enemy, returning him to the wood pulp from whence he came. I need a positive finish here.

I aim and fire three times with about five seconds in between each. I place the gun down on the sandbags and shift down to the scope to spot my shots. Two hits to the left shoulder, one to the bicep. Well shit! I hit the target. I guess that's something. I was aiming for the heart.

I return to my weapon. I peer through the scope and focus in on the head of my target. Headshots are the hardest of all. You can miss the target completely in three directions. If you miss a torso shot, there's still a decent chance you might nail them somewhere, at least slowing them down. A headshot requires the utmost calm, expertly controlled breathing, and hands both like a brick and like a feather.

I'm steady, the crosshair is true. I place my finger on the trigger. I inhale and exhale quickly three times then take in one long, slow breath. I exhale just as slowly. When my lungs empty, I pull the trigger just once. Again, I place the rifle down and hit the scope. I panic for a second thinking I missed completely, but at second glance I see the frayed edge of hole that perfectly matches where the left eye used to be. I move my face away and quickly back to double check. Confirmed. Perfect shot, right through the fucking eye.

I throw my right fist into the air. "Yay!"

I look over to Vick. He is already looking my way. I get to my feet and point down to the target.

"Right through the eye," I say.

"How many times?" Vick asks.

"Ummm ... one."

"Call me when you can do that shit consistently," Vick says, unimpressed.

I wave him off. Fuck him. I did awesome. Greg will appreciate my progress. I turn to him. He's standing right next to me.

"Hey, Teach. Right through the eye. Good, right?"

"Great progress, Josey. Keep at it. We'll make you a

marksman 'fore long."

"Thank you." I turn back to Vick and stick my tongue out at him. He shakes his head, rolls his eyes, and goes back to shooting.

Caleb stands up and walks over to a cooler near my area that is filled with bottles of water. He opens it and grabs one.

"Isn't this fuckin' fan-tastic?" Caleb says to me but loud enough for everyone to hear. "I mean, Jesus. We're gonna get to blow people's fuckin' heads off. Righteous. Righteous."

"Easy jackass," I respond. "You don't have to be a maniac about it."

"Fuck that," Caleb says. "I'd kill your grandma if somebody paid me enough."

"Whoa, Caleb," I yell. "Over the line man."

"Maybe you're in the wrong line of work princess," Caleb says.

He's just trying to push your buttons, Josey. Let it go.

"Maybe you're a nutcase," I say.

"C'mon. Seriously? This shit doesn't get you a little jacked up?" Caleb asks.

"Not really."

"It's not like we're going to have control over the contracts ultimately. Could be to take out a prominent CEO, a drug lord, hell, a bus full of fuckin' snotty, rich kids. You won't know, but you'll have to do it. I'm just choosing to embrace it. Like I said, maybe you shouldn't be here buttercup."

Greg steps over to us. "Hey. We don't kill kids dipshit."

"I was just generalizing," Caleb responds.

"Just watch it," Greg says. "That kind of talk'll get your ass kicked out of here."

"Sir, yes sir!" Caleb shouts as he mockingly salutes Greg.

Greg is not amused. He marches to Caleb and puts his right hand around his throat, his left hand right up onto Caleb's balls, immobilizing him.

"I have told you mutts repeatedly not to call me sir," Greg says looking straight into Caleb's eyes. "I could snap your neck right now like a chicken bone or rip your sack off like plucking a cherry from its stem. Any doubt I could do that?"

Caleb does his best to shake his head. His face is red.

"Do ... not ... fuck with me recruit," Greg barks in his best drill sergeant cadence. "I won't warn you again."

Vick has moved to a position next to me. I'm sure we're both thinking about intervening to keep Greg from killing him but we hold off.

Greg releases Caleb from both places and steps back.

Caleb moans and crumbles to the dusty ground, his hands on his balls. He chokes some air into his lungs, coughs. His eyes are watery and bloodshot, his face beet red.

"Let's get things put away and get ready to head back," Greg says. "You've had enough for one day." He grabs the cooler and takes it to the SUV we arrived in.

Vick goes to Caleb and offers a hand to help him up.

Caleb quickly swats it away. "Get away from me." He rocks to one side and struggles to his feet using the sandbag wall to brace himself.

"Fine," Vick says, throwing his hands up. He walks away. Halfway to his shooting spot, he stops and turns back. "Ya know, you might need some of us one day. Probably not a great idea to piss away every relationship around here." He continues on to pack up the weapons and supplies.

Caleb doesn't respond. With a stiff upper lip, he does as Greg has instructed.

I do the same, all the while wondering what the hell just happened. How does a guy like Caleb even get accepted for training with that kind of mindset? They've made it clear from the beginning the kind of business they run here. Caleb certainly doesn't fit the profile. Not exactly sure I do either. Time will tell. I know my sniper skills need to improve or I won't be doing jack-shit.

# 18

Day Thirty-eight
Wednesday

Madame K's Office – 9:15 am

Madame K is partially sitting on the edge of her desk, hands on the edge, feet on the floor and facing the door. Ollie and Dina are standing in front of her, behind the guest chairs.

"So, let's start with Tech Ops," Madame K says. "Where do we stand?"

"Dak-ho and Emily are standouts, for sure," Dina says. "Mohinder is great, maybe the best of all of them from a technical standpoint, but he doesn't do particularly well under pressure. Might be an issue. Remmie, of course, as you know, has already been dismissed."

"Any ideas on ways we might break through Mohinder's issue?" Madame K asks.

"I don't see any," Ollie offers. "It's been over a month. Every time he is put under an extreme time constraint, his performance plummets."

"I see. Dina, give me odds on whether he'll come around in the next thirty days. You're best guess."

"Some people just don't do well when they feel threatened.

He definitely has both feet firmly planted on the bad side of that. As far as a percentage chance he succeeds here with another month of training, I'd say less than twenty percent."

Ollie nods. "I don't think it's a stretch to say it might be more like one out of a hundred. Considering we're only going to let two candidates move forward after training anyway, I really don't see a reason why we shouldn't just him bounce him now."

"Dina, you see it that way?" Madame K asks.

"If forced to make a decision right now, yes."

Madame K stands up and walks around to the other side of her desk. After sitting, she picks up the receiver to her office phone and presses a button on the base. "I need you to call Li Xia. Code E on Tech Ops trainee Mohinder. That's all." She hangs up the phone. She takes a quick sip of tea from a white mug.

"Now on to our other recruits." Madame K leans back in her chair. "Ollie, you mentioned last night you had some concerns with Caleb. Please share your thoughts."

"As you know, they went off site yesterday to begin real world shooting, and when they returned, Greg stopped me to talk about Caleb. Apparently, the guy keeps making jokes about killing busloads of children and taking out grandmas, if he were paid enough money. Just very unsavory comments that rubbed Greg the wrong way."

"I've also had similar concerns about him," Dina says. "He's never said those exact kinds of statements in our sessions but he's alluded to his complete lack of moral boundaries. I've certainly had my eye on the situation."

"I'm a little confused as to what exactly the conundrum is," Madame K says. "Last time I checked, our function is to facilitate contracts for assassination. Murder. Kill. End life."

Ollie has a look of confusion. "Yeah, but the kind of people we take out is a far cry from taking out a bus full of children for no reason. That's psychopathic. And I don't like that word. Murder. We don't do that."

"No matter what sugary-sweet words you choose to coat

this thing, the result is the same," Madame K says. "I grant you, the child thing is a little distasteful, but Jesus, Ollie, we're not out there selling Girl Scout cookies. Since when did you become such a goddamn humanitarian? You hate everyone."

"I'm hating you right now," Ollie rebuts.

Madame K and Dina are both taken aback by the boldness of Ollie's words.

"Ollie has a point here," Dina reasons. "On the macro level, we can all see the benefit of this organization, but at the micro, we do need to exercise discretion. There's a fine line between the people we kill and the people we are."

"I can't believe what I'm hearing here. Your attitudes are changing about this work, and I don't think I like the direction they're going in." Madame K pulls her chair forward and takes another sip of her tea.

"We have a purpose here, and I refuse to believe this work should ever be done without a conscience," Ollie says.

"Killing with a conscience. You oughta put that on a bumper sticker," Madame K quips.

"Come on you two, let's bring this conversation back where it belongs, on the recruits," Dina pleads. "We have a decision to make here, and this pissing contest is not helping. We can have a deeper philosophical debate some other time. It sure as hell sounds like we need to."

Ollie rolls his eyes and sighs.

"Fine," Madame K says. "Dina, lay out our choices here, plainly."

"By process of elimination, we can say Vick is the only recruit that easily passes all phases. He's an excellent marksman with military discipline and leadership. Has a true sense of duty and responsibility. Physically, he's a specimen. And ... Nazar has given him an A minus for his part. He moves on, no question."

"Do you agree with that assessment, Ollie?" Madame K asks.

"Yes. He is the standout recruit."

"So, what about Caleb, aside from the fact that he rides

some imaginary line between altruistic assassin and cold-blooded murderer?"

Ollie starts. "His recon skills are good, rated B plus by Nazar. He's exceptional with all the weaponry he's been introduced to. He came in with a short military background, grew up in Montana, hunting, fishing, living off the land kind of family."

"Yes, skills wise, he would do fine," Dina adds. "It's really his mental state that bothers us."

"Okay," Madame K rushes to the next topic. "What about Josey?"

"Remarkable veteran level recon skills, even without our help," Dina says. "Can handle her own physically. Resourceful, street savvy."

"There's still work to be done on the firearms part," Ollie adds, "but she's coming along. Her biggest issue will be in her head. Until we put her to the ultimate test, we won't know if she can pull the trigger on a hard target. And she's rebellious. Probably the most likely to disobey a direct order."

"I agree with Ollie's assessment," Dina says. "It's really a tossup between Caleb and Josey, for very different reasons."

"And I've already made my objections about Josey before she even arrived here, just based on the issue of her parents," Ollie adds. "If she were to find out what happened to them, fit will hit the shan, you can bet your ass on that."

"Yes, yes," Madame K dismisses. "You seem to be the only one here concerned about that. Gives me pause with you, Tolliver." She looks him square in the eyes and with the most serious tone says, "Watch your step on that. I, more than anyone, know the risks."

Ollie stands down, silent, his lowered head and slack shoulders saying all.

As the organization's psychiatric specialist, Dina cannot help but analyze the tension between Ollie and Madame K, particularly Madame K's defensiveness. Dina is tempted to back Ollie but decides to leave it alone for the moment.

"We'll leave a decision on this for another day. See me

again in a week about it." Madame K settles back in her chair and turns to the window, already in deep thought.

Dina and Ollie leave without another word.

# 19

Day Fifty
Monday

Vick and I stand across from one another, our fists up and at the ready. Until now, we have sparred, light contact, self-defense type stuff, but today we have been instructed under pain of death to let each other have it. I doubt this will go well, for any of us.

The strength and endurance training has been intense but worth it. We all feel stronger, lighter on our feet, agile, ready to handle any physical obstacle we might encounter on the job. The key now is to keep at it. That was the first part.

The second part of the Dean's program is combat training. Like I said, we've touched on it, practiced the techniques, did some Jujutsu and Kempo karate. All three of us have participated in our fair share of scraps, no doubt, and from personal experience I've had no trouble taking down unsuspecting nitwits three times my size. This, however, is different. I'm competing against someone whose skills match or exceed my own, and he's fully expecting me. We have no weapons, no trusty stun guns, just our skill and our might. I'm nervous. I'm sure Vick is shaking in his disco boots. Yeah right.

Caleb is off in the corner, casually spinning the pedals on a stationary recumbent bicycle. The Dean is standing five feet from us, centered, a stopwatch in hand, a finger at the ready.

"Okay," the Dean alerts. "Within three minutes, one of you better be on the ground. Ready!" Three seconds pass. "Begin."

It's obvious we both feel a bit stupid. He doesn't want to hurt me. I desperately want to hurt him. Oh, the dances we'll do. I need to clear my mind now, focus on what I need to do. If I've learned anything from my time here at the Kill Academy it's that my full attention is the bare minimum required for me to have a chance. Greater people than myself have fallen short for lesser transgressions.

"Sorry, Josey," Vick says.

"Cut the chit chat and fight!" the Dean yells.

I take a half step back to let Vick know I won't be the one to strike first.

Vick throws a right jab at me. I lean left and dodge easily. We bounce around in a semi-circle before he takes another jab at me, this time making light contact with my arm where it meets my shoulder. He backs off some.

I seize the opportunity and distract him with a wide-swinging left hook, which he easily evades, only for me to drop down with a fierce right leg floor sweep. The hard contact with the side of his calf sends him careening to the floor with a thud.

I pop up and bring my foot to his throat, which he grabs. With all my strength, I cannot hold it in place. He twists my ankle and throws me aside with relative ease. Pain radiates through my bad shoulder but I shake it off. I'm on my feet in three seconds. Vick wastes no time doing the same.

"Good, good," the Dean says as she slowly circles us. Caleb has stopped pedaling, his interest growing as the intensity increases.

I can see in Vick's eyes that he was surprised to be on the ground so quickly. I doubt he'll underestimate me a second time.

We're facing each other again, fists at the ready. Vick takes two bounce steps toward me then shifts his body to the right. I land a left hook in the side of his rib cage but too late to realize he gave up the shot as a distraction. Vick lands a right hook square into my left jaw. The force and surprise of the impact spin me around and down to the floor.

I open my eyes to find the Dean standing over me.

"He really knocked the crap out of you," the Dean says. "Lucky you didn't lose any teeth, though you do have a big bruise on your cheek to contend with." She offers me a hand and pulls me to a sitting position.

I gently press on my jaw with the palm of my hand. My face has its own heartbeat.

Vick passes a small, soft, blue ice pack to the Dean, who then hands it to me.

The icy chill feels good.

Caleb emerges from behind Vick. "He knocked your ass out!"

"Shut up, dipshit," Vick says. "You okay, Josey? I got you on that one."

"I'll be fine. You won't be so lucky next time."

"I have no doubt about that," Vick says.

The Dean pushes Vick aside. "Always the diplomat. You think your targets will feel bad?"

We all get the message. She can see in our eyes that we do.

"All right you misfits, we'll call it a day. Vick and Caleb will go tomorrow. And I want to see more intensity."

"You don't have to worry about that," Caleb says.

Vick gives Caleb the evil eye. "You're going down."

"Josey, go down and see the nurse," the Dean commands. "We want to make sure you don't have a concussion."

I nod. I look forward to getting some aspirin and hopefully a short nap. All the energy I had before stepping in the gym has evaporated. I can admit I have some work to do on the combat front. Time to step up my game.

# 20

Day Fifty-one
Tuesday

As promised, the Dean has Vick and Caleb face to face for a takedown. My jaw is still throbbing, so I'm glad to sit this one out. And by sit, I mean literally sit, as in, sitting on a recumbent bike, barely pedaling. I don't expect this one to go as quickly and I have a front row seat. These two are physical equals and it's obvious they desperately want to kick the crap out of each other. If one or both of these guys aren't bleeding by the end of this, I'll be disappointed. I only wish I had a big ass soda and a tub of popcorn.

"Okay men," the Dean says. "Three minutes, all out. Your goal is a takedown. Think Fight Club, not high school wrestling. Got it?"

Vick and Caleb nod. Caleb stretches his neck from side to side. Vick slides his fingers together and pops his knuckles. Is it wrong that I'm getting a little giddy for this?

"Ready! Go!" The Dean steps back after hitting the stopwatch.

Like a heavyweight fight, they dance around each other, inching closer, taking light jabs.

"I'm going to enjoy putting you on the ground," Caleb teases with a quick right cross that misses.

"You're delusional," Vick responds. He plants two quick left jabs followed by a right cross that lands hard to Caleb's left bicep.

"Weak," Caleb says. "I'm gonna fuck you up pretty boy."

"If you two did less talking, maybe you'd actually start fighting," the Dean says. "Two minutes."

From nowhere, Caleb charges Vick as he glances over to the Dean. Like a linebacker blindsiding a quarterback, Caleb dives into Vick, driving his shoulder into Vick's chest. They're both airborne for a split second before hitting the ground with a nerve-twinging thud. The sound sends a chill up my spine.

Vick is too shocked to even move. Caleb takes advantage of his position on top of Vick and starts to pummel him in the face.

After the fourth strike, the Dean moves toward them. "That is enough, Caleb. Yield!"

Caleb is zoned out. He lands two more punches to Vick's bloodied and bruised face.

The Dean is right next to them now. "I said yield!" She grabs Caleb by his right elbow.

Without hesitation, he backhands the Dean across her face, sending her back a few steps. He doesn't even look in her direction. He grabs Vick by the hair and brings his head off the ground only to slam it back down with enough force to concuss the average human being.

I jump off the bike thinking I might need to get involved. The expression on the Dean's face hasn't changed one iota, so there is no telling what's going through her head. Caleb's a big dude but I'm fearing for his life right now. It's one thing to argue with her, but striking her in the face, that is somewhere I'm guessing you never want to go.

Like a shadow, the Dean moves to a position directly behind Caleb, and before any of us even realize what is happening, she launches a series of finger punches to different areas of Caleb's body. If I had to guess, I believe she hit both his kidneys and a few places along his spine.

As if someone had just jabbed a knife into his back, Caleb sits up perfectly erect, then falls down to his left writhing in pain. The Dean rushes over to him, forces her arm around his neck, pulling him upward, and then squeezes with all her might until he passes out. She releases her grip, allowing his body to slump to the floor.

I'm already down on one knee at Vick's side with the goal of keeping him conscious. I turn his head slightly. He spits out blood and mucus.

"Try to stay with us, Vick," I say. "Don't close your eyes." I pull a small towel from my back pocket and use it to dab the moisture from his mouth.

Through the entry door, Ollie and Greg rush in. The hidden surveillance I've always known existed is clearly working.

"What the hell happened?" Ollie asks.

"Caleb lost his damn mind," I say. "Wouldn't get off Vick and then he struck the Dean."

"I've got it under control," the Dean says. "Lock him in his room."

Ollie and Greg each grab an arm of Caleb's and bring his limp body up.

"Madame K and Dina are on their way down," Ollie says as they carry Caleb out of the gym. "I'll be back in a sec."

As Ollie and Greg exit, two of the staff medical personnel come through the doorway, a man and a woman I have never met. I rise up and step aside from Vick to allow them full access.

"What happened to him? And be specific," the male says.

"He was punched repeatedly in the face with a bare fist," I answer. "Then his head was slammed on the ground."

The Dean steps aside and motions me over. I oblige. The medics continue treating Vick. They have him sitting up at this point, which I assume is a good sign.

"Are you okay?" I ask.

"Me?" the Dean questions. "Of course. Took me by surprise, that's all."

"Imagine that doesn't happen often?"

"Almost never. Good lesson for all of us. Crazy people can be quite unpredictable. Must be ready for anything."

I nod. "What's going to happen to him?"

Her eyes tell me everything.

Madame K and Dina enter the gym and walk straight to us. A few seconds later, Ollie and Greg return.

"What the hell happened?" Madame K demands.

"Caleb and Vick were sparring," the Dean answers. "Caleb had Vick down and beat but refused to yield when I commanded it. When I went to pull him off, he struck me. I handled it."

"Lost his damn mind is what he did," I chirp.

Madame K shushes me with a raised hand. I zip the lips. I eyeball everyone. No one reacts to her curtness. I'm still getting used to it. She is the boss, after all, and she sure as hell commands a room. Impressive, really.

"I think we all kind of saw this coming, didn't we?" Ollie says.

"Well, we still had a choice to make up until about five minutes ago," Madame K says. "I guess Caleb has made it for us."

All of them nod in agreement.

Sounds like someone won't be graduating the academy. That only leaves Vick and me. A bit of nervous energy surges through my body. That's not to say that I still won't fail, but one less recruit certainly raises my chances of succeeding.

"Ollie, see to this matter personally," Madame K says. "Let's not have another incident today." With that, she turns and leaves the room.

Ollie gives Dina a look, then they both leave together.

"Well, Josey. It looks like it'll be just you and me today," Greg says with raised eyebrows. "I think we'll go offsite so you can work on your long-range stuff, assuming the Dean doesn't need you anymore."

"By all means," the Dean approves.

"Great. A little nutty around here today anyway," I say.

"I'll grab you from your room in about ninety minutes. Be ready to go."

"Got it."

Greg and I leave the gym and split off down separate parts of the hallway.

Back in my room, I go ahead and switch from workout gear to my tactical outfit. I get in bed and sit up against the pillows on the headboard.

I'm still trying to process what just happened. I knew immediately the severity of Caleb's actions but when the upper echelon of the organization arrived to deal with it, the intensity hit a level I didn't expect. The entire event came and went in the blink of an eye and I was barely involved, short of being a witness, but I'm rattled in a way I can't put my finger on. Sure, some of Caleb's words and actions have done nothing to make me trust him or even feel comfortable around him, but he's clearly unstable. Some part of me wonders if he is more typical of the people in this profession than not. I'm having doubts about all this, and even scarier than that, doubts about my own nature.

# 21

Day Fifty-four
Friday

Vick and I have been called to Madame K's office and we have no idea why. This waiting room is the closest we've been to seeing her office in the nearly two months we've been here. Trepidation? Yes. I can't recall doing anything recently that would warrant a trip to the principal's office. I sure as hell don't like surprises. In my life, they rarely turn out to be good ones.

"So, what do you think?" I ask Vick.

"About what?" Vick answers.

"Duh. The reason we're up here. You're not worried?"

"No. You worry too much. Aside from the Caleb shit, it's been a good week. At this point, I'm ready to take the next step."

"Well, we're the only two left," I say.

"Yeah, and other than continuing to fine-tune our skills, I don't think there's much left to learn without a live test."

I nod in agreement. "That makes sense."

The door to Madame K's office opens, interrupting our conversation, and into the frame steps Dina. "Come on in you two."

Once inside, I am surprised to see not just Madame K but

Ollie and the Dean as well. Dina offers us the seats.

Madame K wastes no time. "And then there were two," she says slyly.

We say nothing in response. The room goes silent for an uncomfortable ten count that feels more like minutes than seconds.

"You've both done well here," Madame K continues. "Aside from a few momentary hiccups, that is. I'm pleased to inform you both that you have graduated phase one of the training."

Relief washes over me but I know we are really only just beginning down this path. I look forward to doing something different, being somewhere different.

"Awesome," I say.

Vick gives me two thumbs up.

"Yes, you have much to be proud of," Madame K says. "Very few ever make it to this stage. The next stage, however, even fewer succeed at but we have the utmost confidence in both of you. The way things work around here, we create teams to achieve what we call Contract Level Alpha kills, or CLAK for short. These kill teams consist of three people – A Point, a Secondary Point, and a Tech Ops person. The Point is in charge of the mission from top to bottom and is the designated trigger person. Tech Ops will assist in providing building blueprints, network hacks, web research, anything along those lines that one might need. The Secondary Point follows the lead of the Point, learning and preparing in the exact same manner, much like the understudy of the lead in a play would, and they must be fully ready to step in and perform the hit should something go wrong. Any questions so far?"

"What other kinds of contracts are there besides CLAK?" Vick asks.

"Well, after a period of time, could be a year, could be five or more, an assassin will have the opportunity to advance to a point where they take on solo missions. Only the best of the best ever advance that far. In fact, we've only had six of them.

These specialists work alone and handle Contract Level Omega kills. CLOK for short."

"CLAK or CLOK. Catchy," I say.

Madame K concedes with a shoulder shrug and a head tilt.

"So, they handle their own tech?" I ask.

"Yes, but a veteran level Tech Ops person does some initial work that gets included with the dossier that is given to the assassin. From there, they are on their own. As you can imagine, it requires a tremendous set of skills."

"When do we find out what the teams are?" I ask.

"There's one more stage to pass before that happens," Madame K answers. "Each of you must partake in a mission as Point. We need to see you demonstrate your ability to finish the job. You would be surprised at how many recruits we lose at that spot."

"So, how will that work exactly?" Vick asks. "Are we talking a real live target here?"

"Yes. Each of you will get a separate mission as Point. Secondary Point will be Amatto. I'm sure you've met him wandering the halls. Tech Ops will be handled by either Mr. Skinner or Ms. Hines. It is a pass or fail situation."

Vick and I exchange smiles of concern.

"We've been training for this for months," I say. "I guess it's time to put up or shut up."

"Indeed," Madame K says with a nod. "And don't fear. You'll be guided and assisted through the first one. The utmost care will be taken to see that you do well." She glances to her watch. "I really have nothing else, so if you two would like to go with Li Xia and Dina, I'm sure you're anxious to begin the prep. Two weeks from today, everything should come together for you. Good luck." She rises from her chair.

Dina leads Ollie, the Dean, Vick, and myself to the cafeteria. Vick and I sit across from the Dina and the Dean, Ollie stays on his feet, I suspect because he doesn't intend to stay long. He's an imposing figure, arms crossed, and damn good looking, if I must admit. Tall, dark, and handsome.

Cliché? Yes, but that facial structure, those bitable lips, and that voice, better suited for radio than as the number two of this organization. As a boss of mine here, I will do my best to keep these feelings in my pants. I may have been crossing my fingers as I said that.

"Can I ask a question?" Vick says.

"Since when do you need to ask a question about asking a question?" the Dean snaps back. "What is it?"

"So, if both Josey and I pass, will we be on the same team?"

"Yes," Ollie answers. "That is the goal, to have at least two of you move on from the training. We are looking to promote Amatto to solo status. His team lost a member recently so we either need to replace that team member with one of you, or create a whole new kill team and allow him move forward."

"Wow," I say. "What happened to the other team member?"

"That, Josey, is privileged information," Dina says.

"You guys are absolutely no fuckin' fun around here," I say.

"Wouldn't you rather hear about the mission you're about to take on?" the Dean asks.

"I guess. All right, give us the goods."

"This is where I leave," Dina says. "Mission details and prep are for Li Xia and Ollie, but we'll speak again soon, prior to your actual missions." She leaves.

"Vick, if you want to come with me, we'll go to my office to get you familiar with mission protocols," Ollie says.

"I guess that leaves you and me, Dean," I say.

The Dean gets up from her chair. "Follow me. It's time to show you how things are truly done around here."

The way she said that terrifies me a bit. I guess it's time for the meat and taters of this meal.

# 22

First Mission

After two weeks of preparation and as much firearms training as I could squeeze in, the day has arrived. My mission, should I choose to accept it. No wait, that's not right. I cannot refuse a mission. Dem's da rules. Once I open the dossier, I must complete the mission or I'll be in deep do-do.

The man that is going to see the bad end of all this, Martin Burney, is a former Wall Street guy who apparently fucked over a bunch of people on some investment stuff during the housing crash of 2007. One of those clients turned out to be the wrong client, Mr. Hadley Worthington. Mr. Worthington lost a shit-ton of money in his dealings with Mr. Burney, but what Mr. Burney didn't understand was the background of the man he had dealt with, more specifically, his ties to Northern Ireland mob families. When Mr. Worthington found out how bad Mr. Burney had royally fucked him, he called in a favor to one of those Irish families, and voila. Here I am.

A question did pop into my head. Why didn't the Irish mob just do this deed themselves? Apparently, when there is a clear and obvious connection back to them, even the modern-day mob plays it smart and hires a professional. My how things have changed.

The truth of Mr. Burney's actions took years to be discovered, but when it comes to fucking with rich people's money, there is no statute of limitations. And despite the fact the lost money was peanuts compared to Mr. Worthington's overall wealth, the slight is unforgivable to him. Steal a million or steal a dime, there are some people you just don't cross.

The basics of my team's prep for this mission was simple enough. The dossier contained a cover page with a name, date of birth, and last known location by city and state. There were several color photos of the target. Also included in the file were specific location markers with small maps - various places where the target might spend time - his home, work, local hangouts, family and friend's houses.

From there, it's the duty of the Point to fill in the gaps, find all the little details that will help bring focus to the target's behaviors to make his every move as transparent as possible. Having that information will assist in picking the right time and place to perform the final deed. In some cases, the target must appear to have died in their sleep, some it doesn't matter, some they never want the body found. We can handle any of those scenarios. In the case of Martin Burney, they want him gone-gone, which means dead and never found. It also means there can be no witnesses to his death. And I don't mean us getting caught, I mean anyone seeing him go down or finding his body. If we are so unlucky, the witness or witnesses get gone-gone too. That is considered a partial failure by my organization and we must work hard to avoid that. Should there be a crowd that we can't easily dispose of, the Point might be the one on the wrong side of the execution. The organization would disavow, a lone gunman situation created, complete with manufactured motives. That is why the prep is so critical. If there is one part of this we can't fuck up, that's the one.

Cover sheet:

Name - Martin Edward Burney
DOB – 06/07/1971
Loc. – Trenton, New Jersey

Photos show a white man, receding hairline that is brown
and gray mixed, what there is of it. His eyes are brown. He's
thin, maybe six feet tall. In each photo, he's wearing a suit,
but not what I'd call expensive ones.

I spent ten days on recon with this guy, scouting him. At
his home, he lives alone and is single, but he was married
once upon a time. No pets. No kids.

The local pub he frequents, Sully's, is busy on ladies' night
Wednesday, walleye fish-fry Friday, and Saturday, because,
well, it's fucking Saturday. He sleazes around the small groups
of women with bad pick-up lines when he's not entertaining
his work crew with tales of his big money Wall Street days
and truly awful jokes. He goes home alone every time. Even
as big a douchebag as he appears to be, I almost feel sorry for
him.

He eats mostly carryout from a Thai place, a pizza place,
and burgers on the go. He hits a small-time IGA grocery
store for frozen meals, chips and salsa, twenty-four packs of
canned beer, a half-gallon of almond milk, and various
cookies and donuts from the store bakery.

His employer, Merrick Investments, is a small financial
management firm that works mostly with middle and upper
middle class clients with small amounts of money. I imagine
this place is the best he can possibly do after that housing
crash mess. He had to lay low after all that, his reputation
tarnished in the big city. Across the bridge and away from
Wall Street, no one knows who the hell he is.

Amatto and I drove to Trenton. We bought a shitty used
car to get there, something we could easily dispose of after
we're done, a process I'm intimately familiar with. I've been
told that on the rare occasions where we need to fly, we will
travel to a city near where the job is supposed to take place,

then get a car and drive to the final destination. We'll be much harder to track that way. When flying can be avoided, we do so.

We've been staying at a seedy and filthy hotel. Cash only. Quite a bit of the clientele is the Lady of the Night variety. The rest tend to be as unsavory as they come. I'm not worried. Nothing I haven't dealt with before. Besides, I have Amatto. On the surface, he doesn't look like a tough guy, but he could disarm and have most anyone on their knees in a matter of seconds. Just like people will always underestimate me because I'm a woman or I'm small, people would never expect him to be so skilled and strong. BAM! Your weapon is now his weapon and your legs have been swept from underneath you like they were made of paper.

It's strange to be out in the world again. I miss the simple things: traffic, people walking about, the smell of coffee shops and the waterfront, weather changes, waking up without an alarm. I almost feel free. Almost. We're not allowed to engage in any non-mission related activities. Dina's words, not mine. So, I won't be taking off to visit the zoo or catch a movie, as wonderful as those distractions would be. It's go time. This is my final exam for the Kill Academy. All the prepping and studying I've done for months comes down to this one test, this one act, this one life. I end him, my training will be complete. Can't get any simpler than that.

Amatto has had some great insight for me. He doesn't say much but when he does it's always astute. One night while we were sitting in our hotel beds eating pizza, he could sense my contemplation about the upcoming deed. Without looking at me and between bites he said, "There's no middle ground on the first one." I had no idea what angle he was going at. I glanced over to him but his eyes stayed on the TV. He continued, "It will either come really easy or be excruciatingly difficult."

I pondered those words for a few minutes. I admit, I have been leery to the idea of actually killing someone, on purpose, for money. I wouldn't have joined the academy to begin with if I didn't believe I could be trained and pushed to do it but there is a reluctance that remains. Amatto doesn't usually give unsolicited advice. He must see something in me. I hope it doesn't manifest in the way he thinks it might. All I can do is prepare the best I know how and count on the team to assist me when needed.

On the Tech side, no real support has been needed. They prepared the dossier, but otherwise, Marty has had no involvement. I've been informed that is a rarity. In most cases, we will lean on the tech person for more than we realize.

For this contract, Mr. Burney is to be killed, his body never found. To the rest of the world it will be as if he just up and disappeared one day. What does that require from me? Ambushing him at home on some night after he has been to Sully's.

During the weekdays while Mr. Burney has been at work, Amatto and I have staked out his house and neighborhood. The house is a mid-century single story, nothing fancy and not likely updated since the eighties. The yard appears to be mowed frequently but the landscaping lacks flowers or ornaments, kept as simple and low maintenance as possible. No surprise there. Mr. Burney doesn't seem the green thumb type.

There's no fence, which has made it easy to tour the property. Downside – no privacy from the prying eyes of neighbors. The house on the east side is also single-story, and that helps. The bushes and trees that line the property edge give us enough cover. It is occupied by a young working couple with predictable schedules. The house to the west, however, is two-story, husband, wife, and a four-year-old child, so we avoid that side. Their schedule is also predictable. They both work and the child is taken to daycare every day. The major variable is the kid. Kids get sick. They have to go home sometimes in the middle of the day. We're watching that carefully.

For Mr. Burney's house, the back door leading to a

mudroom and through to the kitchen is the easiest to enter. We picked the lock and entered without trouble that first day. For some reason, I expected the place to be a serious bachelor pad, chock full of empty pizza boxes and crushed beer cans, but no such luck. The place was picked up and orderly. Not overly sanitary but good enough to bring home a date, should he be so lucky.

There are eight windows in the house and all have curtains or blinds. That's super helpful. I'll have no trouble getting in, staying hidden, and doing the deed here.

We also scouted Sully's, Merrick Financial, the IGA, Thai Cuisine, and The Pizza Place. All of them were quickly eliminated as nab points just based on their locations and the number of people always around.

I had thought about using a lure to get him away from his normal places to somewhere much more isolated, similar to how I dealt with the Battle Boys. The shortest distance he would have to travel from his life bubble would have been twelve miles, which in my opinion seemed too far to not be suspicious.

I am Point on this mission, so the final choices are mine. His house is where I have decided I will do the job. Amatto did not participate in my decision making, although, if asked, he would give me an honest answer. He agreed the house was our best chance of securing Mr. Burney without prying eyes.

Let me set the scene. It's Friday night, late. Mr. Burney is at Sully's hanging and drinking with his co-workers. I'm here in Mr. Burney's living room waiting for his car to pull up. When he does, I'll hide behind the front door and surprise him by throwing a plastic bag over his head. This seems strange to me. I always envisioned myself sitting atop a high-rise building, peering through a scope, and pulling the trigger as the unsuspecting target walks down the street. You know, just like in the movies. But nope, I'll be standing behind the front door with a green vegetable bag I swiped from the produce section of the IGA. Reality is turning out to be far less glamourous and a hell of a lot more work. I need to use a damn sniper rifle. This living room shit is way too intimate for my taste.

I'm fighting the boredom as I wait by rotating my time between cell phone games and nerding on the net. Amatto and I were both issued throw away phones for the mission, luckily with some pre-paid data. I'm pretty sure I've taken a hundred buzzfeed.com quizzes since I've been sitting here. Amatto shared a few techniques with me to stay awake. The big one is don't sit still for too long unless you absolutely have to. I've been getting up every fifteen minutes to walk around, do some stretching, a few jumping jacks. We are discouraged from using energy drinks or pills, and instructed to go easy on the caffeine as well. Can't have the jitters or a major energy crash while trying to take someone out. That would be no good. I've been told, eventually, if I graduate the training, the organization offers a supplement to help calm our nerves, described by Amatto as a close relative to Ritalin. I insisted I wouldn't need it. He smirked, looked me dead in the eyes, and said, "You're gonna need it. Everybody ends up needing it." I believed him.

Making me jump from my seat, the headlights of Mr. Burney's car pierce the front room windows, passing their rays across the room from west to east. Adrenaline pushes my heart rate to an uncomfortable level but settles down as I stand patiently behind the door, taking slow breaths. I slide the plastic bag from my back pocket. I'm in full black gear and I'm even wearing a ball cap. I also opted for a cheap pair of gas station sunglasses.

I hear the car engine idle for thirty seconds until he finally shuts it off. The driver side door squeaks open. A few seconds later it slams shut, which worries me. It's loud enough that it could've woken someone in the neighborhood from a dead sleep. His feet rustle across the ground, steps staggering. He's tipsy. Probably make this easier.

He's at the door. He's fumbling around with his keys.

My own heart rate rises. I get the sensation of losing a

single breath. I stay calm.

He manages to insert the proper key, unlock the door, and push it open. He steps just inside the door and pulls his key from the lock, tossing the keyring on a side table near the door. He attempts the light switch above that table. Up. Down. Up. Down. Up.

I killed power to the lights earlier. I smile.

"Damn CFL bulbs!" Mr. Burney scoffs. "Supposed to last like ... seven years ... god damn it," he stammers.

The time has come for me to act. If I wait any longer, it's only going to get more difficult. Do it. Do it, Josey.

Mr. Burney uses his left hand to flip the door shut without turning around. He takes one step forward.

I'm still in the corner. He hasn't noticed me yet. If he turns around right now he'd see me, even in the dark. He's maybe four feet from me at this point. I can smell the booze, the fried fish, and oddly enough, strawberries. I assume someone spilled or barfed a daiquiri on him.

Before he can get too far, I seize the moment. Three quiet steps. A hard kick to the back of his left knee. I have the green plastic bag in my hand.

Mr. Burney yelps and collapses to the ground, right onto this ass. I imagine he's too drunk to think straight but the adrenaline rush might give him a little clarity. Must act fast.

I quickly throw the bag over his head and pull it tight to his face, cinching the open end behind his neck. I use my left knee and my body weight to apply pressure to his spine, pushing him to the floor. His right cheek is now on the ground. He's squirming. He can't do anything with his arms. He's lost control of the situation. The bag alternates from being sucked in to being blown out, each one more desperate than the one before. Moisture builds on the plastic. I feel the tension in his body release. I'm surprised at how easy this is turning out.

I let go of the bag. I don't know why. He's passed out but he's not dead. I don't have any clue why I let go. My mind is screaming at me to finish it. My body refuses to acknowledge.

Apparently, it's not so easy after all. I start rationalizing, from all sides. *This guy's a creep, doesn't mean he deserves to die. He's a scumbag. He ripped people off. He's someone's son, brother, friend. He's a waste of space in this world anyway. If allowed enough time and opportunity, he'll probably end up date-raping someone. He's never actually physically hurt anyone though. Why'd you join the organization, Josey, if you can't do this shit? Why Josey? Josey. Josey. Josey.*

"Josey," Amatto shouts, shoving at my shoulder.

I snap back to reality and look up at him. I jump to my feet.

"He's still breathing," Amatto says.

"I know."

"You've been in here a while. What's the fuckin' problem?"

"I don't know. I just couldn't do it."

"You were like, twenty seconds away from finishing." Amatto throws up his hands. "What the hell?"

"I ... don't ... know. I panicked. I have doubts. I just need a minute."

"We don't have a minute. You've been in here too long as it is. We still need to get his body out of here and every second we're here is another second someone might see us. Finish it. Now!"

"I can't!"

"Goddamn it, Josey! You're fuckin' this up. Big time. It's not gonna be good if I have to step in."

"I know, I know. I just don't see the whole story here and it bugs me."

"What story?"

"HIS story. I can't come to grips with why death ... for this asshole ... is suitable punishment for being bad with investments."

"Not your problem. This is your assignment. Time to finish it. What it's not the time to do is have an ethical stick up your ass."

"I can't think right now."

"I'm giving you ten seconds or I'm gonna wrap it up for

you."

"Please!"

Amatto kneels beside Mr. Burney. "Five seconds."

"I ..." I shake my head.

Using both hands, Amatto lifts Mr. Burney's head from the ground about eight inches. "Last chance."

I gently shake my head, begging him no.

With the snap of his wrists, Amatto breaks Mr. Burney's neck.

I suddenly have a brick in my stomach.

"You really fucked this up."

I place my hand over my mouth, then slide it down my face. All the training and torture I've been through, gone in a microsecond. "Shit."

"Where's the bag and the trunk?"

I point to the hallway.

"Damn, I wish this guy had a garage." Amatto runs to the hallway and returns with the large, black body bag I had brought with me. He lays it flat on the floor next to Mr. Burney's body. "Grab his legs."

I jump right to it. We lift his body onto the unzipped bag. Amatto circles the body as he pulls the edges of the bag up. Finally, he seals the long gold zipper until Mr. Burney disappears.

"I'm sorry. Fuck."

"Don't be sorry to me. You're going to have to answer to Madame K. I wouldn't want to be in that room."

"You can't possibly be all that intimidated by her. Not now. You've been around a while."

"Oh, I forget sometimes what it's like to be a noob. Hang on a sec, I'm gonna get the trunk." Amatto disappears down the hallway and returns with the large trunk I also brought. "Help me with this."

We work together to fold the body bag in half and squeeze it into the trunk. And when I say squeeze, I think I really mean cram. We weren't gentle. I'm certain we snapped the spine, broke a few rib bones, and crushed a few fingers and toes. Amatto closes the lid and takes a seat on top to catch his breath. I stay on my feet.

"You got the hand truck?" Amatto asks.

I opted to bring a collapsible hand truck, hoping to make it super easy to wheel Mr. Burney right out to the car. The trunk is small enough that no one would suspect there is a body in it, and what reasonable killer would take the time to load such a thing into a car with a hand truck? Hopefully, no one will see us anyway.

I go to the hallway and return with it fully expanded. Amatto stands and moves aside, allowing me to load the trunk. Without saying anything, I go out of the front door empty-handed and just look around to make sure the street is quiet. I see Amatto has parked the car right behind Mr. Burney's. I go back in.

"We need to leave," Amatto says.

"I know. I was checking to make sure it was clear."

"This is my mission now. You're assisting. Under some circumstances like this, I might have had to kill you. You understand that right?"

"Yes." The severity behind my lack of action is settling in. Jesus, I'm an idiot.

"Grab that thing and follow me out. We need to be quick."

I follow his orders and within five minutes we're on the road. After loading the trunk, we went back in the house briefly to make sure nothing was out of order. To anyone wondering, it would appear he came home from the bar, threw his keys on the table, then up and disappeared like a speck of dust in the wind. Amatto informed me that on some missions it would be necessary to set up a more elaborate way to explain a person's disappearance. On this one, it didn't matter. Sometimes, we'd take some luggage, clothing, keys and cell phone, and the car to suggest the person went somewhere and never returned. No need on this one. The contract only required he disappear. They didn't care how it looked.

We're driving out of town to a location in the middle of nowhere where we plan to burn the trunk at an old hunting cabin in the woods. We discovered it while looking for the perfect place to complete the second phase of the contract. It didn't look like anyone had used the cabin in many years.

"Am I totally fucked here? You're not gonna gone-gone me, are you?" I ask as we watch the fire burn from inside the car, far enough away that we can monitor it but not be seen should someone arrive.

Amatto snorts and chuckles.

That worries me. I've never seen him so much as smile. I might be a dead woman. Oh Christ.

"No. I'm not gonna fuckin' gone-gone you. Madame K might." He sounds completely serious.

"I think I'm going to be sick."

"Do it outside if you need to. You puke in this car I *will* kill you."

We sit for a minute and watch the flames glow and wave and flicker in the night. It's so easy to get mesmerized by a fire against the dark. There's an almost meditative quality to it, like I could throw all my worries into the blaze and free myself of their burden.

"I take it you don't know much about Madame K, really?" Amatto asks.

"Only what I've been told, which hasn't been much. I know she commands a certain respect that even Ollie and the Dean won't challenge."

"How do think someone like Madame K gets to the top of an organization like this one?"

"Honestly, I've never really thought about it. I assume she's got a checkered past full of killing puppies and kittens. Probably hates cake and ice cream, big fan of Putin."

"Cute. But no. Well, maybe, but never mind. She helped found the organization like thirty years ago. Before that, she did this assassin shit on her own and did it well."

"Really? Wow. I can't really picture Madame K getting her own hands dirty."

"Yeah. In fact, she did it so well, she gained quite the reputation around the world. She was responsible for igniting at least two military coups, and you're probably too young to remember, but that U.N. Ambassador from Zimbabwe that was killed supposedly in a roadside bombing thirty-three years ago," Amatto stops and just nods a few times. "She single-handedly changed international politics for years. And she was your age then."

"Damn. Sounds like she did some interesting things. But tell me, how does that make her so scary *today*? I don't get it."

"Ah. That international stuff is what ended up putting her in charge of the organization, but what really made her an infamous assassin was her brutality."

My eyes go wide. She comes off as a mean ol' bitch but I can't see her going all *Mortal Kombat* on people. "If you're trying to scare me, it's working."

"You need to know who you're dealing with. Let me share a story Ollie told me after I first joined."

32 Years Ago – Unknown Location in the Middle East

Kucharski watched the horizon as the sun hit the dunes, the haze like the world was on fire. No matter the mission, the place, the circumstance, she always took the time at dusk to reflect and center herself. Once day turned to night, her operational training took hold, the work at hand her sole focus. She had planned for weeks, meticulously plotting and designing, leaving nothing to chance.

Being a foreigner in the Middle East made it difficult enough, but being a woman, well ... that made it especially challenging. Anyone who caught sight of her immediately became suspicious. During recon, she worked mostly at night, wore disguises, slipping in and out of places like a black cat in the shadows.

The contract would have been onerous, perhaps even the kind of mission that would have warranted a Navy Seal team, should it have been government sanctioned, but Kucharski was alone. She understood the high-risk nature of assassinating a man who hid behind the concrete walls of a large compound, guarded by no less than six men on the exterior, possibly more on the inside. The five-million-dollar payday, however, made her decision easy, by far the largest of her short but impressive career. She didn't know it at the time, but a few years later, that money would seed the organization she is now in charge of.

She approached the compound from the south. She had set up a small camp a mile and a half away, secluded, with the intention of walking through the desert after dark to reach her destination. Her outfit - tawny and coffee colored tactical. She had blades hidden in twelve locations of the outfit, five small firearms, a set of night vision goggles, a satellite phone, and in her hands, a Colt M16A4, heavily modified and complete with a grenade launcher she used for smoke bombs.

One hundred meters away, she stepped toward the east corner of the compound, a bit of an approaching blind spot she discovered in recon. She figured she could easily get to within thirty meters without detection. From there, she would create a diversion, if necessary.

On one knee, she scanned the darkness through the night-vision goggles, locating the four guards that stood firm at the front gate. The only other entrance was another smaller gate on the east wall. It was barricaded and impenetrable, thusly, it was never guarded directly except for the two watchmen that continually walked the entire perimeter. Those two never crossed paths. They circled the wall walking clockwise. When one of the guards started walking from the east gate to complete his circle, the second guard would reach the gate about two minutes later.

Kucharski turned her focus to the side gate. The rotating guard came into view quickly. He took a few moments to look out into the darkness, stopping for a few seconds in the direction of Kucharski. She mirrored the stillness of a lion on the hunt. The guard moved on with no hint of his role as the prey.

She had little time to waste. Hunching low, she ran to the back corner of the wall, her large firearm out in front. She hit the wall and peeked around the corner. The guard was nearing the northwest corner, so it was time for the second guard to appear on the opposite. She slung the rifle to her back and slid to the back wall, crouching down to stay out of sight. Patiently, she waited for the guard to reach her. The second he hit the corner, she unsheathed a large knife from her thigh and thrust it straight up into the man's gullet, just behind his chin. He let go the grip on his assault rifle as Kucharski removed the knife. He placed both hands on his wound, his efforts to yelp failing.

Kucharski kicked the legs out from under the man, sending him face down onto the ground. His heart stopped beating a few moments later. She dragged his body just around the corner, out of sight of the other guard who would shortly come back around.

Just as predicted, the guard arrived at the side gate, this time not even bothering to give a thorough look around into the surrounding desert. When he reached the corner of the wall, Kucharski performed the identical knife killing she had accomplished on the first guard, and with similar results. She instantly squashed the idea floating around in her head that this job was going to be easy. She knew better than that.

With the bodies stacked along the back wall, she carefully stepped around the large pool of blood on the ground where both men had been stabbed. She noted how black the blood appeared under the gleam of the moon.

Kucharski made her way along the wall to the front corner of the compound. With a quick glance, she confirmed there were four guards, all heavily armed, all big guys. They weren't going to voluntarily disband, so a straight on hit wouldn't work. If she started firing, she might've gotten one or two of them, but then chaos would likely have ensued. She would need a distraction to separate them, and soon. They would grow suspicious in the coming minutes when they realized the roaming guards were MIA.

She moved away from the wall about five feet, directly out from the corner. The contrast of her outfit with the wall would make her visible, but against the backdrop of the night desert, she would be harder to spot. Down on one knee, she aimed her assault rifle at the group of men, then shifted the barrel about twenty-five degrees south and another twenty degrees into the air. She pressed the secondary trigger, launching a smoke bomb that landed and exploded one hundred feet away from the guards.

All four jumped from their casual conversations to red alert. Two of the men, with guns raised, immediately walked toward the billowing smoke. All of the men's eyes were fixated on the landing spot. She was pleased the distraction had the desired effect.

One of the two remaining guards at the gate went for his walkie-talkie but Kucharski couldn't have that. She set off as fast as she could. On the run toward them, she fired two quick shots with the assault rifle, hitting the guard trying to radio, once under his left eye, once in the throat. Blood and bone sprayed the wall behind. The other guard turned and looked back just in time to see the man slump and fall dead to the ground. Assuming the shot came from out in the desert where the smoke originated, he turned back around and yelled something to the others. It was then, out of the corner of his eye, the man saw their attacker charging from the east.

Kucharski threw the rifle over her shoulder and pulled a small silencer equipped pistol from her right hip, quickly planting three shots in the guard's chest before he even knew what he was looking at. Like a jumping spider trying to immobilize a cricket, she threw herself at him, sending both of them to the ground. As he choked on his own blood, she fired two more shots into his head to make sure he wouldn't be getting up.

Quickly, she turned to the gate and fired one shot, shattering the padlock. With her head on a swivel, she turned her attention to the desert and the other two men. The smoke had dissipated, the two guards ready to fire on her. She jumped to her feet, holstered her pistol, and flew through the gate, seamless and smooth in her movements.

The men charged forward, guns at the ready, firing off a few shots that blasted stone and stucco from the exterior wall. They never got close to hitting her.

Kucharski didn't go far. Four feet inside the compound, she brought her rifle back around and turned to the gate. It was pitch black inside the walls making it impossible for them to see her but the moonlight outside was just bright enough for her to target them. Standing still, she needed just one shot each to take the remaining guards down only a few feet from the gate.

She paused, listening for any movement around her. The courtyard was as quiet as it was dark. She turned to the house, which was some thirty feet away, and watched for movement or lights. Nothing. Her own weapons were virtually silent but those couple of shots the guards got off might have drawn attention. From what she could tell, the people of the house were undisturbed.

There were no blueprints for the house that she could find, no plans for the compound at all. She had managed to get her hands on a thermal imaging device but only for two days. From what she could ascertain, the man and wife of the house slept in a room on the northeast corner of the single-story home. A child, between eight and ten years old based on their size, slept in a room on the northwest corner. No one else came and went from the house unless called upon by Kucharski's target – Dr. Kambiz.

This doctor, a chemist by trade, had gotten himself into the devious business of chemical weapon formulation, and some of his recipes had been used on unsuspecting civilians in Iran's never-ending conflict de jour. That wasn't nearly enough, however, to get anyone's attention in international politics. It was only when a top cleric in the government of Saudi Arabia suffered the loss of eight family members in a dirty bomb attack that a personal vendetta was born.

Somehow, the Saudi Arabian government had traced the development of the chemicals used in the attack back to Dr. Kambiz, and from that point forth, he would be held personally responsible for the eight deaths. With no movement on the military or United Nations fronts, the cleric took matters into his own hands and made the contacts necessary to engage Ms. Kucharski's services. For the cleric, there was no price too steep. The five-million-dollar number thrown out by Kucharski, a dollar amount she expected would be outright rejected and negotiated down, was accepted without hesitation. She would've shit a solid gold brick if she could have. She only wished she had asked for ten.

Kucharski entered the unlocked front door of the home, because let's be honest, with a ten-foot concrete wall surrounding the house and six men guarding it twenty-four hours a day, there wasn't much point in using the good, old-fashioned deadbolt. The layout was straightforward. To the left was a kitchen and dining area, to the right was a gathering room and space for prayer. Directly opposite the front door was the double wide entry to the hallway where the two bedrooms flanked a large bathroom. It was plain as day that the accommodations were not the Kambiz family norm. They were in hiding and under protection. A doctor and chemist of his stature within the Iranian regime would be wealthy and living like a king. Kucharski wondered why the family could not have been protected in a more lavish living space than this. Perhaps, she thought, this was temporary while other arrangements were being made. Either way, it didn't matter anymore. His time had run out.

She crept to the hallway, a pistol in each hand. Her hopes were to cut down the doctor and get the hell out of there before the wife and child even realized what had happened. To the right she went. The door to the bedroom was closed. She holstered her left-hand weapon and inched the knob as far as it would go before slowly pressing the door inward. After releasing the knob as carefully as she had turned it, she pulled the second pistol back out.

The bed was centered on the north wall. Even in the dark, it was clear the doctor slept on the left side of the bed. Both were sound asleep. The only illumination was the clock radio with glowing red numbers.

Kucharski took a step into the room. In the middle of taking another, her attention was thrust back to the hallway by the sound of a child's voice uttering the Persian word for mommy. Kucharski spun around to find the daughter of Dr. Kambiz a few feet away.

When the girl discovered the woman standing before her was not her mother, she let out a blood-curdling scream.

"Shit," Kucharski whispered. She glanced back to the bed to find both the doctor and his wife scrambling to wake up. *This just got seriously fucked up.*

Her training and survival instincts kicked in. She whipped her head back around to the child. A lamp on the doctor's nightstand switched on. With almost robotic precision and determination, Kucharski fired two shots into the chest of the girl, sending her backwards and onto the floor. The human part of her didn't want to, but the protocols in her line of work dictated that no witnesses could remain. Age and sex played no part in the equation.

The wife screamed and burst into tears, blubbering words Kucharski couldn't make out. Dr. Kambiz was now on his feet, unsure what to do. He had no weapon and thus no way to defend himself. Kucharski made direct eye contact and she could see in his soul that he understood why she was there. His eyes begged for leniency. He placed his left hand out toward his wife and gently shook his head as if to ask for her safety.

Not an ounce of doubt entered Kucharski's mind as the bullets flew from her guns. The wife crashed against the wall with one head wound and two in her chest. She slid down to a sitting position, her head dipping forward, a wide streak of blood on the wall trailing her down. Dr. Kambiz decided to charge but didn't get a second step in before the spray of bullets spun him back and over to the bed. His body flopped hard onto the bedding, his blood soaking through right down to the mattress. He attempted to get up, his torso elevating slightly before falling back down, lifeless.

Kucharski bolted from the room, leaping over the child's body like it were nothing more than a deep puddle to avoid on a rainy day. With empty hands, she ran out of the compound and into the desert until she reached her camp. From there she made contact using a satellite phone to an ally that would help get her back across the border and into Turkey. She would fly from Istanbul and out of the Middle East to several other European airports before ending up back in the states.

As far as assassins go, she had already been well-respected and feared, but with that contract, her very name became a word of dread. Going forward, she would simply be known as K.

"That did not help me, AT ALL," I say.

"The point is, she's no one to be trifled with, but she's not your enemy right now. You failed a training exercise. Failed might be too soft. You royally fucked up a training exercise. I can't tell you how the leadership will react for sure, but let's just say, you might not be out yet."

I'm surprised to hear him say that. I was under the impression this was a pass or fail situation. Pass and you move on, fail and you go home, or worse. "How could I not be out after that debacle?"

"I don't know, Josey. I can't say for sure and I really shouldn't be saying anything. You'll just have to see what happens when we get back. Don't assume anything. That's all I can say."

My mind races with possibility. If I'm allowed a second chance, do I even want it? Maybe this assassin thing just isn't for me. The lifestyle could be nice though – the travel, the money, I could really do right by the Leers. I close my eyes and throw my head back. What the hell have I got myself into?

The fire has dwindled to smoke so we exit the car and walk over to the ash pile, probing it with sticks to make sure there is nothing left for anyone to find. Amatto is satisfied, and just in the nick of time. The horizon is beginning to glow. We wanted to be gone by the time the sun came up and it looks like we'll just make it.

Amatto pops the lid from the gallon of water he brought, dousing the ash to finish it off. Once the final hot spot fizzles out, we return to the car. The plan is to drive all the way to Albany, ditch the car and find another, then head back to HQ.

# 23

Madame K's Office

"Looks like you might've been right about her," Madame K says.

Upon their return to headquarters, Amatto filed a detailed report that was now sitting on the desk in front of Madame K. Dina and Ollie had copies of their own but they had also spoken directly to Amatto.

"Couldn't finish the job. What a disappointment," Madame K adds.

"Like Ollie suspected, she can't see past her own motivations to the bigger picture," Dina says. "I'm not sure there is much we can do with her."

"Amatto didn't complete his first either," Madame K says.

"Yeah," Ollie answers, "but that was an execution mistake, not a psychological one. And ... he's refused to give his personal opinion on whether he believes Josey will come around or not."

"We can just cut her loose and team Amatto with Vick," Dina says.

"I want Amatto on his own. He's earned it ... and needed." Madame K flips to a different page in the report and quickly reads something on the page.

"Of course," Dina says. "But with no viable second from

this batch of recruits for the team, what choice do we have?"

Madame K strokes her chin. "I have ... an idea I've been tossing around in my head. I think we can all agree that for Josey to get over the hump it needs to be personal to her. No horse in the race. What if she had a mission that might affect someone she cares about?"

Dina gives Madame K a confused look. "How would that even be possible?"

"I don't think I like where this is going," Ollie says.

"If she can see and feel the benefit of doing her job, she'll have an easier time seeing that same result for others. Once she does, I firmly believe she'll fall perfectly in line. Her skills are too impressive not to be thorough here. I'm not going to waste her talent because of some psychological hang-up."

"Again, how can we accomplish that without ... ya know, manufacturing a kill?" Dina asks.

Madame K's stone cold face says it all.

Ollie is seething, about to boil over. "This is bullshit!"

"Watch it, Tolliver," Madame says. She points at him. "Watch it."

"I don't understand this place anymore. What you're suggesting is way over the line with me." Ollie is gripping the arms of his chair so tight, his knuckles have turned white.

"With all due respect," Dina says, "nothing like that has ever been done around here. Would you please spell out exactly what you have in mind? Maybe we can't see what you see."

"It's simple, really. We hire someone to kidnap one of the Leer kids, make it look like he's seeking payback on some racket their father got into. We set up a fake contract to take out the kidnapper, only Josey doesn't know he's kidnapped the kid. We'll create a story. When she gets there to do the job and discovers the kid, she'll have all the motivation she needs."

"Do you know how crazy that sounds?" Ollie asks. "A million things could go wrong. If Josey found out we faked the whole thing, she might wig out and kill us all. She loves that Leer family like they were her own siblings."

"Sometimes, Tolliver, I don't feel like I know you anymore," Madame K says.

"Perhaps you never have," Ollie retorts.

"We are in the business of training killers so we can complete contracts. Nowhere is it written how we should go about doing that."

"I agree with Ollie. It's risky, Madame K. Josey was a crapshoot from the beginning. We all knew that. I vote no."

"Luckily, this isn't a fucking democracy." Madame K rises from her chair and slams her hands down on the desk. Ollie and Dina jump in their seats. "I MAKE THE GODDAMN RULES AROUND HERE!" With her hands still planted on the table, she says, "I've already come up with the details and emailed them to Li Xia for plan prep. Get on board or get out." Her voice has already returned to its normal tone. She calmly lowers herself back down to her chair.

They don't bother arguing any further.

As they walk to the Dean's office, Ollie and Dina converse quietly.

"What the hell just happened in there?" Dina asks.

"She's lost her god damn mind, and her ethical compass is just plain fuckin' broken. We don't kill innocent people, not unless it can't be helped, and only as a last resort. We start down that road, we don't come back."

"I'm inclined to agree but what can we do? She's made her choice. Her attachment to Josey is clouding her objectivity. I take some solace in assuming the unlucky target of this phony mission will be some criminal misfit that won't be missed by anyone. But still."

"I don't know sometimes, Dina. I've had thoughts lately."

"You're not thinking about leaving, are you? Or worse yet, the M-word?"

Ollie tips his head to the side and gives Dina a shoulder shrug, a half-hearted grin, and raised eyebrows.

"Wow. I need time to process all this, and I'm sure as hell

not ready to talk about that at this point."

Ollie releases a big sigh. "I'm not either, not really. I'm just pissed. She's changed recently. She used to listen to us. I learned everything I know about this business from her, including the bloody end of it. She was always the most unique talent, unparalleled. Even at her age, she could probably still take me."

"She still listens to us. When this Josey mess is settled, we'll just have to have a deeper conversation with her, when nothing is on the line."

"Yeah, and get my ass killed over it."

"Ollie, you're like a son to her. She'd never do that. It's part of the reason why she's harder on you than anyone else around here. Your relationship is different to her, special."

"Maybe. You don't think there is something else going on with the whole Josey thing that we're not seeing, do ya?"

"If you mean other than the obvious one, then I'm not sure. Josey has clearly affected her in a way we've never seen before. Might be worth looking into, quietly. If she's holding onto a secret, could explain her behavior."

"I'll poke around a little, see if I can dig something up."

"Just be careful, my friend," Dina says with a gentle pat to the back of Ollie's arm.

"Of course."

# 24

I hate being locked in my room. I'm seriously going stir crazy in here. It's been two hours without a peep from anyone. Amatto has never given me any reason not to trust him, so when he gave me the impression I would not be eliminated for failing the test, I felt better, but I still haven't decided if there is any true honor amongst the thieves around here. Best case scenario is that they let me leave, no harm no foul. Worst case, I'm gone-gone.

I'm still processing the fact that Amatto killed Mr. Burney and I helped move his body out to the middle of nowhere to burn it. The smell for that first twenty minutes will never leave me. I can't even compare it to anything I've ever experienced. Let's just say, it made my eyes water and my stomach churn. Amatto had offered me something like a vapor rub to put under my nose but I refused. I didn't want to appear weak, even after he told me that even the strongest among us have their limits. Regrets, regrets, regrets.

There is a double knock at my door. I stay put. The lock pops, the door opens, and in walks Vick. I'm more excited to see him than I will ever admit to anyone.

"How ya doin'?" Vick asks.

"It's been a tough couple of days. How about you?"

"Went well. I'm officially in. I've been back for a few days, waiting to see what happened with you."

"So, I take it you've heard about the spectacular fashion in which I failed my live test?"

"Yep. What happened? I mean, Jesus. We went through all this training and in the end, you just couldn't seal the deal?"

"I know. Don't be a dick about it. Think they'll give me a second chance?"

"I do."

"Think they'll let me go to the bathroom?"

"Of course. You're about ready to meet with the Dean. I asked if I could talk to you for a few minutes beforehand. If they give you a second chance to complete a mission, do you actually think you'll be able to pull it off, really? Because if not, I would seriously consider just leaving instead."

"I hope so."

"Better do more than hope. You go into that office with the Dean, you best be confident about what you want or they might just bounce your ass."

"Thanks, Vick. I appreciate you coming in to talk to me."

"I think this place will better with you in it than without. Go get it done."

I nod.

"Go to the bathroom, then I'll walk you down."


I'm sitting before the Dean in her office. It's just the two of us. Surprisingly, there is very little tension in the room. I fully expected to come in and get my ass chewed but it doesn't feel like that's about to happen. I could be wrong. The Dean is a mysterious woman, probably full of enough secrets to fill a hundred walk-in closets.

There's a brown folder on her desk, her hands resting lightly on it. If I were under arrest, that folder might contain my rap sheet. But I'm a wanna-be killer coming off an epic fail of a contract, so that folder is probably forty pages worth of my mistakes in excruciating detail, sure to embarrass the fuck out of me.

"This folder contains the beginnings of another mission," the Dean says as she taps the folder. "When the preliminary information is gathered, your last chance to join this organization will be ready for you. I assume you want another chance?"

"I do," I say with confidence, even if I'm not sure I truly believe it.

"You are free to leave right now, go back to your old life of scraping by on the streets as a hoodlum. You sure that's not what you want?"

That cut a little deep. Not sure I deserved it. "I'm sure." I can't hide on my face the anger building inside, and she's too perceptive not to see it.

"Good. You should be angry."

Damn my terrible poker face. "I'm angry at myself. I thought I could do this."

"Whatever your hang-up is, leave it behind. Just remember the kind of people that end up in our claws. They are as far from innocent as they come. I've seen your file. I know you've helped people. This just happens to be a permanent way of dealing with someone - no checkups, no blackmail, just done. Flip the switch. You won't always see it, but what we do here often saves others down the road."

I take in a deep breath and nod. "I got it. I know I can do it. I will do it."

"Good. There are some people in this world that are bad right down to their bones and can never be anything but. Then, there are people like you and me, people molded by unfortunate circumstances. We can have a positive impact. We can do the world a favor. If you can draw that line and trust in the process, you'll be fine."

"Thank you. I can. How long before the mission is ready?"

"Be another week, maybe ten days. Just continue training until then, especially with firearms. I have a feeling this one will not be as simple as the last. Now go take a shower, take a nap, and try and relax for the rest of the day."

I leave the office and head for the bathroom, the moments of my failed mission weighing heavy on my mind.

# 25

Dina's Office

"So, we gonna break down my deeply ingrained psychological hang-ups?" I ask.

"Nope," Dina retorts. She hasn't made eye contact since I walked in. She's fixed on her laptop screen and it's making me crazy with impatience.

"How about hypnotizing me? My subconscious is screaming to get out. That little devil will tell you some things." I know I'm being a snarky ass. I can't help it.

She remains unruffled, my light-hearted banter not fazing her one bit. Her mind appears to be somewhere else, but she called me in here, so I have no idea what is up. She finally turns and addresses me.

"What do you know about your parents?"

"Wow. Cutting right to it. Shouldn't I lie down on a couch or something?"

"I'm being serious here. What do you know or what do you remember?"

"Honestly, I don't remember anything. I was four when they disappeared. Never found.

I assume they were declared dead. That is all I know." For some reason, the phrase gone-gone comes to mind. This training is really getting to me.

"You ever think about what might have happened to them?"

"From time to time, but that was nearly twenty years ago. If they ever showed up on my doorstep, I'd be kind of pissed actually. Like, where the fuck have you guys been? Do you know the shit I've had to deal with because you weren't here? No hugs and kisses from my end."

"Interesting. How curious are you to know what really happened to them?"

I give her a funny look. "Obviously, it's a huge mystery, so of course I'm curious." She's pressing this pretty hard. My curiosity is now aimed at her. "Is there some reason you're asking me this now? I've been here for months and this is the first time you've asked about my parents. It's kinda weird."

"Being part of this organization has benefits, resources. The kind of resources that might allow someone to gather information that is otherwise not available. Assuming you make it past your final training, you might be able to utilize those resources. But you didn't exactly overwhelm anyone on that last mission. Has some believing you lack any real motivation for success."

"Like you?"

"I didn't say that."

"You're acting different today with me. What else can I assume?"

"You can assume whatever you like. I've always thought you had what it takes to be successful here but you seem to keep one foot here and one foot planted in your old life. One of them will win out, one way or another."

"Well, I'm a classic underachiever with a severe decision making disorder. Maybe the problem is that you guys just aren't very good at evaluating talent. Marcus, Arnoux, Caleb ... me. Only wonder boy Vick is left. That's not a very good pass rate."

"But it is about average. Of each recruiting class, only one makes it, occasionally two."

I'm trying to get a rise out of her but she is unflappable today. Not that she's ever been anything but. I guess I'm just in a mood and it's clear she is too.

"Just to ease your mind, I do want to be here and I fully intend to conquer my next mission."

"I'm glad to hear that."

"And I understand your point about resources. I don't need any further motivation, but I'll certainly add it to the list of reasons, help me get fired up."

"Good."

"Any other familial issues you want to dive into while I'm here?"

"No. We're done for today. You can go."

"A pleasure as always." I get up from my chair to leave.

"Josey," Dina says as I reach the door. "This talk about your parents, please keep that between us."

"Okay." I thought the entire parentage conversation was weird to begin with, but as I think about how Dina's been acting today and now this secrecy request, I'm thinking something is up. Suddenly my spidey-sense is tingling. I leave without saying anything else. I have a feeling this conversation will be rattling around in my head for a while.

# 26

The dossier cover page reads as follows:
Name – Terrance Grayson
DOB – 4/29/1986
Loc. – Baltimore, Maryland

The photos show a black man, just under six feet tall. The basic research has revealed he works out, spent some time in prison for grand theft, lives in the basement of a friend's house, and is heavily involved in running drugs and money. His location will make it easier for me considering the Greater Baltimore Metro is my home turf but it also troubles me. What are the odds my second training contract would be there? I'm trying hard not to make more of it than it is. Maybe the organization is giving me the best opportunity they can for me to succeed. Still strange.

Amatto has joined me as backup and is once again completely hands off unless asked. Tisha Hines is handling Tech Ops this time around, and I must say, she's damn good at what she does. When I asked her for a blueprint of the warehouse I'm scouting, the place where I believe Terrance is making pickups, she had that shit back to me on my phone in like forty-five minutes. And without even asking, she provided a schematic of where the cameras are located and how the building is wired with a homemade ADT type security system fed to a private offsite server. Obviously, they can't go through an actual security company considering what they're doing in that warehouse. Their private system, however, makes it much easier to undermine, if needed.

We drove to Baltimore in a beat-up Jeep Grand Cherokee. We're staying at a crappy motel within walking distance of the warehouse. When the recon is finished, we plan to ditch the SUV and find something else to go home in.

The contract is the easiest type for an assassin. How the target dies is irrelevant and it's okay if someone finds him dead. The one caveat on this one is that there could be an innocent person being held by the target, and the contract specifically requests this person be freed and unharmed. The complication, if any, may come from the fact that I have to help someone escape, which really means I can't take this fucker out from a distance. No sniper shots, no picking him off on the street, no car bombs.

Why Terrance needs to be taken out is being withheld for security reasons. I'm told that it happens from time to time. The organization knows the full details but the team does not always get all the information for their own protection. I can understand that. I'd feel better knowing but nothing can be done about it, so I'll just have to deal.

Terrance isn't going to be the only one in the building and I have no intention of killing every damn person on my way in and out. I'm going to have to be stealthy, a ghost. My basic plan is to enter through a basement window off the alley. It's just big enough for me to squeeze through, and because of that, unwatched.

Once inside, I will sneak my way from floor to floor until I reach the fourth story, the place I have discovered Terrance picks up his supply of pot or meth or whatever. It varies depending on the week. There is nothing being produced in the warehouse, it's more of a temporary storage space. This helps me. If say, meth was being cooked there, security would be much more stringent.

To get out, I'm just going to find the back door and walk out like I belong there. If the door guy gives me shit, I'll put him down, but hopefully that will be the only collateral damage.

I'm not that familiar with this end of town. It's not the mean part of the Baltimore area I'm used to. The neighborhood is slowly being transformed from old warehouse district to a loft apartment filled, trendy, single-person haven. Some blocks, however, are still in bad shape, and this is one of them. Regardless of the location, I still have to be careful not to be recognized by a local. I can't afford to be tied to this area. I must be invisible, quiet and dark like a mid-winter evening sky. I admit, being home, I've had serious temptations to peek in on the Leers. I won't, but damn have I been tempted.

So, I've been staking out Terrance and the warehouse for eight days now. He comes every Wednesday and Saturday for his pickups. The time he arrives is not always consistent which will force me to wait around for him to enter before I make my move.

I haven't seen or heard anything in regards to this captive Terrance might have. That worries me. In this line of work, we've been taught to avoid surprises. One surprise can end a mission, end your life. The more we leave up to chance, the more likely we'll be to fail. I can't fail on this one.

I'm in a vacant building across the street from the warehouse. The room on the second floor I'm in was once an office of some type. Not sure what happened, but they left the furniture and artwork, though now it's all mostly broken and dusty. There's a blue desk chair with a wheel missing but I'm choosing to stand and keep watch out of the window. Don't know if some hobo pissed himself on that chair, or perhaps worse.

I can see the street perfectly even though it's dark out. Most people pull down the alley to the left of the building and park in the back. It's Saturday and Terrance should be coming around in his silver Acura soon. The car stands out with its red LED strip lights on each side. This wannabe race thing he's got going on really spikes my douche-o-meter.

And there goes the needle. I spot the Acura coming down the street. 'Bout damn time. I'm sick of waiting for this asshole. Time to prove I can do this job.

I'm wearing all black except for a pink hoodie underneath my jacket so I can appear less suspicious for my casual walk out of the back door. I'm also sporting three knives and four guns on my person, not to mention a few other tactical supplies.

My plan is to get in, waste Terrance, grab the kidnapping victim, and come right back here to let shit cool down. I have asked Amatto to arrange for transportation, preferably a minivan or something where the rear is private. He's waiting nearby for a phone call from me. He can be here in under a minute. Should something go wrong, we can get the hell out of here quickly but we'll be exposed. The better option is let some time go by and leave once the area has calmed down.

I pat myself down for a last check of my equipment and to doubly make sure I have my phone. If shit goes bad, I'll press and hold the number one to get Amatto engaged prematurely. If that happens, my short stint in the assassination game will be over about as quickly as it began. I'm trying hard not to think about that.

I exit the building and walk casually down the street a few hundred feet before crossing over. There's no one around, a stray car or two, but no pedestrians. I walk back toward my intended location and veer off when I hit the first alley. The large dumpster is by the basement window I intend to squeeze in, right where I need it.

I duck behind the dumpster and get a good look around for prying eyes. There is no movement, no lights, nothing. The only outdoor security camera is on the front of the building near the other alley, the one people use to get to the rear parking. This side has a fence about halfway back so vehicles cannot pass through. It's just wide enough for a waste disposal truck to back in, empty the container, and pull right back out.

During recon, I came to this window and made sure I could open it. There was some dried paint that needed to be sliced through but it was unlocked. With a little muscle and a thin pry bar, I managed to pull it open. It was much easier this time around. I pop it right open with little effort.

I go through the opening head first and wiggle, falling to the ground on my hands. The drop is further than I remember from my first visit. I wrench my left wrist some but it's nothing I can't handle.

The room is pitch black. I pull a tiny flashlight from my utility belt and twist the end. A bluish, white beam shines forward leading me right to the rickety wood staircase that leads up. The oak treads creak as I ascend. My breathing is shallow. With my right hand, I pull a .9 millimeter, just in case. My first time here the door was unlocked. To make sure it stayed that way, I removed the strike plate so if someone did lock it, I could easily chisel out the wood around it to get out.

I have no way to know if anyone is on the other side of the door. I listen and hope for the best. Not an ideal situation but there's no choice.

I press my ear to the painted door, chipped and worn from time. I hear absolutely nothing but my own pulse. The door opens to the end of a hallway and just below the staircase I will use to get to the upper floors. The stairs almost perfectly divide the building in half from back to front.

Slowly, I push the door open until there is just enough space to crawl out. I stay low, my flashlight off and back on my utility belt. To my left is a wall, to my right, the hallway and staircase. I see no one. The only light is a dim yellowish one from somewhere above the stairs. I follow the wall until a post and some balusters appear. I peek around the other side of the stairs and see an identical hallway, a door at the end that leads to the back of the building, and a brute of a man sitting on a fifties era chrome-framed and gold fabric dining room chair. He's fully engaged with his smartphone and has what I would describe as a hand cannon on his waist. This is the guy I'll have to face on the way out.

I climb the staircase until I reach the fourth floor. The

second and third floors appear to be unused - the furniture, the dust, the random trash all undisturbed. At the top floor, my destination, the hallway to the right is as undisturbed as the second and third floors, so I head to the left. The building is quiet.

There are four doors down this side of the hall. The footprints in the dust all stop at the third door. Jackpot. Good news - if anyone shows up, they're only going to be coming from one place. Bottlenecks are a good thing. I can mow them down as they come at me. Bad news - I have no idea how many people are actually in the room or how heavily armed they are. I know Terrance carries two custom silver, .45 caliber Nighthawks. Nice guns of surprisingly high quality for such a dipshit. Of course, he's probably got all the *Fast and the Furious* movies on Blu-ray and watches them frequently. Can't win 'em all.

There is light coming from under the door. I'm nervous but prepared. Time to get the ball rolling. Using my left hand, I turn the knob, restrained. I ponder for a moment whether I should just bust in, guns blazing, or perhaps take off my jacket and play the confused little lost girly who stumbled into the wrong building. Damn it, Josey! Stop second guessing yourself. You decided on guns blazing earlier, so that's what you're doing.

I fully open the door and quickly scan the room. There's a table to the left with small silver packages I imagine are bricks of weed. Terrance is standing there transferring the packages one at a time into beige canvas duffle bags. He hasn't seen me yet. There are a few folding chairs on the floor to the right, all collapsed or knocked over. There's a single CFL bulb dangling from the center of the ceiling, sparsely lighting the large space.

Random thought. Who's paying the electric bill in this place?

Almost directly under the light is another folding chair but this one is being used. Sitting there, arms tied behind the back, a black hood over the head, is the person I presume to be the kidnapping victim. I'm startled by the size of the person, clearly a grade school aged child. It never dawned on me, not for one second, that it could be a child. Now that I know it, I'm pissed.

Thankfully, the child is hooded. I can waste Terrance without the child bearing witness.

"Well, what do we have here?" a voice says from behind me. I about crap my pants.

Terrance turns to us.

I freeze, unsure how to react.

"You bring a friend, Sharky?" Terrance asks, seemingly unalarmed by my presence.

I turn and get a look at this Sharky. He's Latino, a few inches taller than me, bald head, and a lot of tattoos including a tiny one under his left eye I can't decipher. He's wearing dark blue faded and sagging jeans, and a plain white t-shirt under a shiny Yankees track jacket.

He gives me a funny look but is also unconcerned about me. Just another example of people underestimating me. Should work to my advantage.

"She ain't with me. You're not supposed to bring hussies around here dummy."

"I'm not a hussy. I'm here to kill Terrance, duh."

They're both confused. They think I'm being funny. The kid starts bouncing around in the chair, mumbling, kicking some. That's weird. The kid is wearing sky blue Converse.

"Oh, shit man," Terrance yells. "She's got a fuckin' gun. Grab her."

Sharky puts a firm grasp around the upper part of my right arm. I swing my other arm around and drive my elbow into the side of his head. His grip releases and he flies backward into the hallway. I face him and quickly fire three shots, one dead center to his chest, the other two hit near his left shoulder. He slumps against the wall. I was hoping for none, but that's collateral damage number one.

I step out into the hallway and take cover to the left side of the doorway. A bullet whizzes by, shattering the wallpaper and plaster on the wall to my right.

I take a quick look in. Terrace has both of his guns out and is now behind his captor. I'm becoming consumed with those blue shoes. Coincidence, I tell myself. Another fucking coincidence on this job. Lots of kids have those kinds of shoes. It's not like they're unique. Can't worry about that right now. With all the gunfire, I'm guessing my friend guarding the backdoor will be coming up the stairs any second now.

I decide to preempt that arrival. I rush to the top of the stairs, and sure enough, there he is charging up. He sees me with my gun pointed. I fire a shot. He ducks down and to the right just in time to avoid taking a slug. He stays low and fires three shots right back at me. That gun of his sounds like a tank firing. I crouch and roll to the other side of the stairs as the wood of the top post and cap shatters around me.

I pull a five-inch knife from my boot. The man has moved back a few steps and is attempting to hide behind the post of the rail at the landing. He's a little pudgy around the midsection and one of his love handles is hanging out in plain view. I heave the knife and it lands firmly in the side of his gut.

He jumps up, exactly as I had hoped, and screams. "Shit!"

I need only one shot to his right temple to end that problem and bring my collateral damage total to two. I've also just freed the exit. I'm genuinely surprised at how easily I'm taking these assholes out, not from a technical standpoint, but from a mental one. I may have turned a corner on this whole assassin bit, or the fact there's a child being held captive in the next room is aggravating me enough to motivate. Maybe it's just easier to kill someone when you know they're trying to do the same to you.

"Warren? You get her?" Terrance yells.

I return to the doorway of room number three and peek in again. Terrance is still behind the kid, one gun pointed at the child's head, the other at the doorway.

"Terrance, I want to talk."

"Fuck you, bitch! Crass owed me money and he's gonna

pay up, one way or another."

Crass? That can't be right. But there's no way in hell some other lowlife in the Baltimore area went by the name Crass. Wayne Leer's street name was Crass. That is coincidence number three on this job. Damn. One coincidence is noteworthy. Two is strange. Three is downright suspicious. I suddenly remember the kid's blue shoes.

"TERRANCE! You need to let the kid go."

"No way! She's my leverage. I want the ten grand Crass owed me or this kid ain't making it outta here."

She? Fuck. This keeps getting worse. I don't know what the hell is going on here but the level of aggravation growing in me is forcing my blood pressure up.

"I don't give a shit about that kid and I don't know anyone named Crass. I'm here for a whole 'nother reason. You've been a naughty, naughty little boy, Terrance." I take a chance and step slowly into the doorway, my gun at my side, pointed at the ground. I don't want him to feel threatened.

"Bullshit. And don't you come any closer or the kid gets it."

I take one step closer. "We both know you're not going to kill that kid. Leverage. Remember?" I take another step. "Let's just let the girl run out of here and then you and I can have a discussion. I know we can work something out."

Terrance is shifty, tense. He might be intoxicated. If true, his reaction time will be a wink slower. Then again, it might make him trigger happy. I don't have many choices here.

He presses the end of the gun to the child's temple. She moans in fear. She might be crying too. "I said don't move. You don't know me, bitch. You don't know what I'll do."

After my sixth step, about halfway to them and within twelve feet or so, I stop. "Fair enough." With my left hand, I feel my backside and verify the pistol is still there. "We're kind of at an impasse here, Terrance, but I want to help. If I slide my gun over to you, will you let the girl go so we can talk in private? Will you do that for me? I'd rather not see her die. I mean, Christ, she's just a kid, but I really couldn't care less one way or the other. I could just plug you both."

He's sweating. He's nervous and unsure. I definitely don't want him to panic and do something stupid.

He pulls the gun away from the child's face, just a few inches. It lets me know he's thinking about my offer. "Slow, super, super slow. Slide it over. Any funny business, she dies."

"No problem." I show him both hands and begin crouching down. I place the gun down and slide it over to just in front of the chair. He'll have to come around to get it. That's to my advantage. "There ya go." I stand up straight again, keeping my hands open, facing him, but near my waist.

Terrance takes the bait and steps around to the front of the chair, and for the briefest of moments looks down to locate the gun before putting his left foot on it.

In those few seconds, I slide my left hand to my back and pull a .9 millimeter from the holster on my waist. I aim high so I don't hit the kid and fire a shot. His right arm flails, sending one of his guns across the room. The kid flinches. A second shot. Terrance stumbles from the impact to his chest, the right lung. He'll soon be choking on blood. A third shot. A little higher this time and right into the side of his neck.

He wants to fight back. He wants to shoot his weapon. He's lost a lot of blood already. He's too weak to engage. He stumbles. On his way to the floor, he manages to lift his left arm, the one with the other gun, and fire off a shot in the direction of the kid. Gravity and his lack of strength throw his aim off, sending the bullet into the ceiling. He hits the ground with a thud, gargling. He lasts seven seconds before his life is gone.

I did it! Part one of the contract is complete. Terrance is dead. Phew. Now to get the kid to safety.

I suddenly realize too much time has gone by. The first bullet flew some time ago. If anyone nearby heard all this gunfire, the cops could already be on their way. Time to get the hell out of here.

I holster my gun and pull out one of my three remaining

knives. I cut the rope holding the child's arms behind the chair and help her to her feet. Time to find out if my biggest worry about this kid is true. I pull the hood off her head. My stomach drops. Evie. I'm mad as hell she's been dragged into all my bullshit, and in the worst way.

Her eyes go wide at the sight of my face. Her cheeks are moist with tears.

"This is gonna hurt." I tear the duct tape from her mouth in one quick swipe.

"Owwwwie!" Evie screams.

"Are you hurt?"

She shakes her head.

"Don't look around too much. It's kind of gruesome in here." I grab her hand and lead her out of the room. "We need to get the hell outta here. Stay behind me."

We begin descending the stairs. I pick her up and carry her past the guy I killed on the stairwell. I return her to the ground on the second landing.

"What's going on, Josey. I'm scared. Did you kill all those guys? Why are you here?"

"It's complicated. I'm taking you home. You're safe now. That's all you need to worry about night now."

I grab my phone and call Amatto. "Pick up on aisle one." I hang up as we hit the first floor.

"Josey!"

"Just keep up. I'll explain once we're safe."

We reach the backdoor. Evie pulls away from me, stopping us dead in our tracks. I turn to her. Her lower lip is quivering. She starts bawling.

"I'm so sorry, Evie. You're safe now." I embrace her, putting her head to my chest. "He didn't hurt you, did he?"

"No," she says through tears. "I just ... don't understand." She sniffs hard and lifts her head. "What did I do?"

"Oh, sweetheart, nothing." I put her face gently between my hands. "Absolutely nothing. This is all my fault, but it's over now. We gotta go though or we'll all be in deep do-do. I have someone picking us up. Let's get to the car, then we'll figure all this out. Okay?"

Evie nods.

"Come on." I take her hand and lead her out of the backdoor. It's dark. The nearest working light is a building over. We run to the left, past douchebag's car, around the corner of the building, and down the alley until we hit the street. Waiting for us and blocking the alley is Amatto in a blue, late model mini-van.

I throw open the backseat sliding door and usher Evie in. I join her, shut the door, and off we go.

"Everything okay?" Amatto asks as he drives us away from the scene.

I still don't hear or see any cops. "We're good."

"Job done?"

"I took care of it. Had to put down two others. Question ... did you know about this?"

"About what?"

"That this fucking contract was complete bullshit. They manufactured the whole thing. There's no other explanation."

"I don't know what the hell you're talking about, Josey. Manufacture?"

"I know this kid, Amatto. I'm from Baltimore. This whole thing was set up, custom made for me. I just know it. I may have just killed three guys for no fucking reason other than to pass my training."

"That sounds crazy, and I don't know anything about that. Doesn't seem like something they'd do."

"You gotta admit, it seems suspicious."

"A little."

"Evie, how long have you been away from home?"

"Just tonight. He snuck in the house and took me right out of my bed when everyone was asleep."

"Well, it's ten 'til four now. We may be able to get you back home before anyone wakes up. Amatto, head towards Johns Hopkins. I'll tell you where to go from there."

# 27

We pull up to the Leer house. It's 4:20 in the morning. The street and house are quiet.

"How'd the guy get in?" I ask Evie before I open the van door.

"I don't know. We went right out the front. It's probably still unlocked."

"What time does Gabby usually get up?"

"About four-thirty."

"Can I ask you a question? If you were in bed sleeping, how did you come to have your shoes on?"

"I saw them by the front door before we left and I asked him if I could put them on. He said yes."

"Oh. Okay. Weird."

"I don't know if you should go in there, Josey," Amatto says. "Probably better to just let the kid go and get the hell outta here."

"Not happening. This whole mission has been one big bunch of horseshit from the get go. I know these people. They're like family to me. I have to explain things."

"That is highly irregular. I don't know how the company will react."

"Come on, Amatto. You've had some time to think about it. There's something sketchy about this one, right?"

Amatto sighs. "Maybe. It's got a funny smell but that doesn't mean it's necessarily rotten. Either way, it's dangerous to fuck with protocol. I wouldn't get in the habit of it."

"I hear ya but bear with me. Stay put for a bit. I won't be long, then we'll get outta here. Please."

"Twenty minutes. Then I'm leaving, with or without you."

I nod. "Come on, Evie. Let's go face the music."

The front door of the house is indeed unlocked as Evie remembered. The house is dark, peaceful. I hate myself for the crap I'm about to bring into this home. I understand this must be the last time I show my face here, assuming I stay with the organization. If I decide to continue helping the Leers, it will have to be done at a distance. Makes my heart ache.

Evie turns on the living room light, then the dining room chandelier. I take a seat at the dining room table.

"Go wake up Gabby. Tell her I'm here and that she needs to come down so we can talk real quick. Don't tell her anything about what happened tonight."

"She's gonna be pissed you're here."

"I know. Tell her it's urgent."

Evie starts to leave but I stop her.

"Maybe go change first and wash your face. You got a little something on ya."

She looks down at her pajama top and notices for the first time a few spots of blood. Her face has a few small droplets as well, and the area around her lips is bright pink from when I ripped off the duct tape.

She heads up the stairs.

I inhale deeply a few times. How did this situation get so FUBARed? I never trusted the organization. This presumed fake contract has done nothing for that. I don't know whether to bail now before I become so infuriated that I do something really stupid, or stick around to reap the benefits that come with being an assassin and just suck it up when it comes to the downsides. Why is this so fucking complicated?

There's a commotion upstairs. Muffled voices. Stomping. Arguing. Gabby appears at the top of the stairs, looks me dead in the eyes, and storms down. She does not look pleased.

I rise from my seat to face her. Gabby walks right up to me and slaps me straight across the face, hard enough that it may as well have been a punch.

"How much more can you put this family through?"

"Please let me explain."

"Evie told me everything."

"Probably not everything."

"She told me enough. Whatever this racket is that you're into, this criminal behavior, you've put us in danger. How can you live with yourself?" Gabby begins sobbing. "They took her right from her bed. She could have been killed, Josey. She says you killed the guy."

"I didn't know about any of that until after the fact. I would never have allowed it had I known. And that asshole left me no choice."

Gabby's sobbing has turned to rage crying. "Your presence in our lives is the problem. First, you tell me you killed our father, then this mess. You're toxic. I want you out of here."

"It was an accident. Your father."

"I don't care."

"He made me promise. His last words were about you guys. He made me promise to look out for you."

Gabby shakes her head. She crosses her arms. She's furious but calmer.

"Will you at least let me explain what happened before you send me away? Please let me do that."

By now, Evie and the twins are standing on the landing of the stairs, clearly instructed by Gabby not to come down.

"I don't know if I can believe anything you say. When I look at your face I see nothing but lies. You come into our lives under false pretenses, then you drop this bomb on us and expect everything to be fine."

"I didn't tell you right away because I knew things wouldn't be fine. I knew you wouldn't care how or why. I just hoped you would. I think of you now as my own family and that somehow made it even harder. There's no excuse though."

Gabby puts a hand over her mouth. She starts lightly crying again. She rubs the tears from her eyes.

"I'm so sorry." I cry with her.

Evie flies down the stairs and damn near tackles me with a bear hug. She's crying too. The twins come down and join us. It dawns on me that Pete is missing. A little part of me freaks out.

"Where's Pete?"

Evie lets go of me. "Band trip," she says.

I'm relieved. "Gabby, can we please sit for minute? I would like to tell you the story of what happened to your dad. I only have a few more minutes then I'll have to leave. Please."

"Kids, sit down," Gabby instructs.

They all file in around the table. Evie sits to my left, the twins across from me, Gabby at the head of the table. I take a seat and begin. I look to each of them for a second. I've practiced the story I'd tell them. Now I have to deliver it. Regardless of how they take it, I have no choice now.

"Full disclosure, I'm not a good person, at least not always. I've been involved in some things I'm not proud of but I don't know any other way to live. The streets are where I grew up, where I learned how to live, where I learned to get by, and that lifestyle is part of who I am."

I swallow hard. "Having said that, I don't hurt innocent people. I do take advantage of people but only ones that are into really bad shit. I leave good people alone. I even help good people whenever I can, like you guys.

"Your dad, whether you realize it or not, was not always a good person either. He got involved with some bad people, and those people took advantage of him. They knew he was down on his luck, that he lost his wife, that he had a family to care for. They offered him a chance to make a lot of money, illegally. The risk seemed minimal to him, like he could easily get away with it, and in return, he could make sure the house got paid for, that you had clothes and shoes and food.

"But with these kind of bad people, one favor is never enough, and they wanted Wayne to do more. He didn't want to. They made him. They scared him with threats of hurting you guys. So, he went on more jobs, and before long, he quit his real job at the furniture store and was all at once lost to the same streets I'm a part of."

I take a quick breath and scan everyone's faces. They are enthralled, motionless, fearful. Time is ticking. I have no doubt that Amatto will leave without me if I'm not out there soon.

"One night, a little over a year ago, I heard about a drug deal scheduled to happen on a Friday night. My plan was simple. Once the money and drugs were exchanged, I'd swoop in and steal the money. The guy on that end was your dad.

"When I saw him, he seemed worn out by life, just tired. He was trapped and wanted out but was too terrified to make a move toward leaving. He worried you kids would be hurt if he did anything, so he carried on.

"The night of the exchange, I cornered him in the building after the other guys left with the drugs. I wasn't going to hurt him but he panicked and drew a gun on me. I needed the money really bad at that point. I pulled a knife. We tussled. I somehow overpowered him. Like I said, he was tired and weak. The gun went off. We were face to face. I didn't feel any pain. His eyes told me everything."

The entire Leer family, and me as well, are teary eyed again. I've got just a few minutes before I have to leave, so I continue.

"I didn't mean to. I'm sorry, I told him.

"He looked down to his stomach. The blood had soaked through his shirt. He had grown quite pale already. He fell out of my arms and slumped to the ground, against the wall.

"Your dad told me that you kids didn't know about the bad shit he was into. He said Gabby won't understand. He asked me to look in on you. He told me he thought there might be some good in me, that your last name was Leer, and that I needed to find you, make sure you're okay. They're good kids, he said. I'm a bad father but they're good kids. Please."

Everyone is crying. I put my head down onto the table and into my arms. I'm bawling harder than I probably ever have. Gabby has the sense to run into the living room and grab a box of tissues. The table ends up with a few large, crumpled white piles.

Our weeping is interrupted by my cell phone going off. I pull it from my pocket and answer it.

"You alright in there?" Amatto asks.

I wipe my nose and clear my throat. "Yeah."

"Two minutes. Okay?"

"Thanks." I hang up.

"I gotta go guys. I hope you can forgive me someday. You might not see me again for a while but I'll find a way to talk to you soon." I stand up and push my chair in.

Evie jumps up and bear hugs me again. The rest of the Leer family gather around us. A perfect and loving group hug from them gives me all the forgiveness I need. I can't stop crying. For the first time, I know I am one of them.

The embrace is short-lived. I head to the door. Gabby is right behind me.

"You guys are safe. Don't worry. This whole mess with Evie was an anomaly and won't happen again. I promise. I'll call you soon from a number where you can reach me if you need to. That way if anything weird happens, you can let me know."

"I don't really know what to say right now," Gabby says. "It's a lot to take in."

"Just know that your dad loved you guys, and though he made a big mistake, his intentions were pure."

Gabby nods.

I turn and leave the house without saying anything else. If Amatto and I don't get the hell out of this area soon, it won't be good.

I hop in the front seat and slam the door shut. I can't bring myself to look back at the house. Amatto can see I've been crying but doesn't ask me any questions. He just drives. For nearly four hours we sit in silence as I process the events of the last few days.

# 28

For the first time, I'm being allowed to enter the Kill Academy without being drugged or blindfolded. Amatto told me on our way here that he has communicated my successful completion of the mission and I have more or less officially graduated. What that means, exactly, I'll find out when we arrive.

It's a ten-story building somewhere in New York City. Which borough, I have no idea. I'm not familiar in the slightest with New York. It's a busy business district, which is ballsy considering the work we do. The illuminated sign above the entrance reads AWT. That must be a front. There's an entrance on the left side of the building to a subterranean parking level. The driver of our transportation is retina scanned to get in. The next steps I take with the organization will decide my future.

After disposing of the mini-van in Trenton and while we waited to be picked up by a company car, Amatto and I had a deep conversation about big picture stuff - the mission, the organization, the leadership, and my place in it.

Amatto relented to my suspicions about the mission. The team-level missions are carefully screened, researched, and prepared before being handed off for execution. He thought the odds of that mission coming around at this time, in Baltimore, involving a Leer kid, and it being my final training mission were astronomical. He started to wonder about the leadership. He now wants answers as much as I do. It makes me feel good to know he has my back.

It's one thing to think something lay afoul but quite another to actually come right out and accuse the organization of manufacturing a mission just to pass a recruit. Though a strong debate exists as to the ethical nature of our business, there is an unwritten code that dictates how we should or shouldn't behave. Amatto is certain this mission, if it were falsely created, violates that unwritten code. To his knowledge, nothing like this has ever been done.

Amatto eventually asked the question, "What's so fuckin' interesting about Josey Baldwin that would make them go to these lengths to help her succeed?"

I couldn't fathom a good answer. As far as I'm concerned, I'm just a street rat with some decent survival skills that they plucked out of the city. I had the proverbial hard knock life in a children's home, a few fosters, sex, fighting, alt-rock, and petty crime that eventually elevated to secondhand grand larceny. Could the organization be desperate for talent? Or is there is some missing piece to this puzzle?

Waiting in a coffee shop for our ride, I asked Amatto if he had any regrets about joining up, and what he thinks I should do if it turns out the entire mission was rigged.

"I have no regrets, per se," he said, "but there are downsides. It gets lonely. Even for someone like me who is introverted by nature. Life in this work is dangerous and it makes it hard to have real relationships with anyone outside of it. Relationships inside of it, well ... enter at your own risk.

"As for your contract predicament, I can't tell you what to do with that. I will say, that generally, the organization does a good thing for society, though I'm sure it's not perfect. I have gotten a sense around the office that the times may be a changin'. I'm not sure what that means yet, but me, you, Vick ... we're the future of the company. If we want things to be run a certain way, we can best do that from the inside. We can guide this ship wherever we like. But if it bothers you too much, you might want to leave before you do something stupid. Otherwise, stick around and see what the job has to offer."

In those words, I heard exactly what I needed to. I'm endlessly fascinated by this job. I don't always agree with the methods, but over time, I may be able to change things to make them better. There's still the mystery of this forged contract. The fact that someone had to sign off on it knowing the Leer family might be put in harm's way boils my blood. Evie had a gun to her fucking head. I can only imagine the psychological damage she'll incur because of it. No kid should have to throw their blood-spattered pajamas in the garbage.

Amatto and I hit the elevator in the parking deck. "I'm going to let my suspicions about the contract rest for now," I say. "Can I count on you to do the same, at least temporarily?"

"Sure. I'll do some poking around though. If I come up with any useful intel, I'll get back with you. Of course, I won't be around much. Your graduation means my graduation too. I'm moving on to solo work. Time for me to get the red envelope jobs."

"Wow. So, if you were on a kill team before now, what happened to the other members of your team?"

Amatto rubs his forehead. "They're dead."

"Oh shit. I'm sorry. What exactly happened, if you don't mind me asking?"

"Maybe another time."

"Fair enough."

The doors open at our floor and we exit the elevator. We split off with a nod, Amatto heading for a debriefing with Dina and the Dean, me to clean up and grab a coffee before a debriefing of my own.

# 29

"Amatto reports you did a great job," Dina says. She's sitting back in her chair, relaxed. She normally sits very erect. She's trying way too hard to set the emotional tone of the room, as if I won't pick up on it. She glances down at the piece of paper in her hand. "Maintained your composure, completed the contract in full, planned and executed perfectly. How do you feel about it?"

"Honestly, I'm still kind of coming down from the high of it. Even though it's been almost a day now, I feel like it just happened."

"Anything you want to discuss about the mission? Anything troubling you?"

"Crazy that it was in Baltimore." I give her a little of what she wants. Oh boy do I ever just want to let her have it, but nope. Not going there.

"Certainly unusual. I heard the kidnapping victim was Evie Leer. Something to do with money her father owed?"

"That was even weirder." I'm going to test her reaction. "What are the fuckin' odds?" I chuckle a little, pretending to blow it off as a big coincidence. "Crazy shit."

Dina has one hell of a poker face. "How'd the Leer family react?"

Nice try, Dina. During our wait to be picked up, Amatto and I fully worked out the stories we were going to tell. As far as anyone is concerned, I never revealed myself to Evie.

"You tell me. I did as the contract instructed. Blindfolded and dropped at home. Then Amatto and I got the hell out of there. I assume she's okay. Should I be worried?"

"Nothing to worry about. Probably tempting though, right? Stop in? Say hello?"

"A little. But this was my last chance to finish training. I wasn't going to screw it up." I have no idea if Dina knows I'm lying.

"Good. How do you feel having to actually pull the trigger?"

"It was easier than I anticipated. Of course, those assholes were trying to kill me too. Lot easier to fire on someone who's firing on you."

"True. Confident you'll be successful going forward?"

"Yes."

"Well, congratulations. You've successfully completed your training and will now become a member of the next Kill Team."

"Thank you. So, what exactly does that mean?"

"The first year, you'll be living and working as part of a three-person team. For each contract you all receive, there will be a Point, a Secondary Point, and a Tech Ops person. Your team consists of you and Vick as alternating Point and Secondary. Emily will be your Tech Ops person. You'll all be moving into a house a short distance from civilization where you'll live together and plan your missions. Assistance from headquarters is, of course, always available."

"Cool."

"This is where the job gets very serious, Josey. Failure is not an option. Your team will get contracts that might be even more dangerous, more complicated. But you'll start making some real money too. In a few weeks, all of you will be given a thirty day leave so you can sort out your affairs, tie up any loose ends in your life. Once you arrive at the house with your team, your movements will be limited for that first year. If things go well, you'll be able to go back to living on your own and will report to headquarters for work."

"So, that house is a kind of test then? See how well we can work without direct supervision?"

"In a way, but you'll be supervised. Surveillance on that property is heavy and state of the art. If there's a squirrel in a tree, we can know it. Doesn't mean you'll be monitored all the time. But there are no secrets there."

"Wonderful," I say with a fake smile. "Maybe I should rethink all this."

"It has a heated pool."

"Aaaaaand ... I'm back in."

"It won't be as bad as it seems."

"Freedom is a tough thing to surrender."

"That's what you signed up for. Certainly, you understood the solitary nature of this work?"

"I did. In the abstract, it's easier to handle. The reality is a bit like a belt tightening around my neck."

"It's only a year. After that, your life will be more normal. You'll be able to get your own place, report to work like any other normal person. Be able to travel to some really cool places too."

"You all really need to print up a brochure. Seeking a life of intrigue and wonder? Want to travel to exotic locales and swim in a heated pool? Want a high-energy job where you can absolutely slay the competition? Come join AWT."

Dina snickers. "You're a riot, Josey. Maybe we should put you in marketing."

"Oh no. That sounds very much like a cubicle job. No cubicles. Oh yeah, I've been wondering. What does AWT stand for?"

"Advanced Weapons Tech."

"Is that a fake business front?"

"Definitely not. It's a very real, highly successful design, manufacturer, and wholesaler of custom weapons and accessories. While it is a front of sorts for the basement level stuff you're involved in, it does operate on its own merits and is quite lucrative. The few times you have been to Madame K's office, that was on the top floor of this building. She's the president of the entire place, not just this end."

"She's kind of a mean one. There's some darkness in her. Sure as hell wouldn't want to get on her bad side."

"She has a tough job. Can't afford to be any other way. Any other questions for me?"

"So, we having a grad party or something?"

"No, but if there's something special you want, like food or drink wise, we might be able to arrange something."

"Cake," I practically bark. "Sorry. Double chocolate cake, a pizza from a local place, not that frozen shit the cafeteria serves us, and ... a few cases of beer."

"I think we can manage all that."

"Awesome. Thanks."

"You're welcome." Dina looks to her watch. "Go get some rest, chill out for a while. Vick and Emily will be around later today for the official team introductions. I'll see about making that request available for tonight so the three of you can let loose a little."

"I look forward to it."

# 30

Madame K's Office

"How'd she react?" Madame K asks.

"Better than I hoped," Dina responds. "She admitted to being a little suspicious, but knowing Wayne Leer's past, she didn't seem too surprised."

"Did you get any inclination whatsoever that she might believe the contract was staged?"

"No. If it's crossed her mind, she's buried it deep enough to keep it from us."

"What about the girl? Is she okay?"

"Yes. Fine, as far as we can tell. Josey didn't say much about her, but I'm guessing she's miffed that the kid was put in danger. But again, she seems to be steering responsibility for the predicament to Wayne."

"Good. I think we found our team then. We'll keep a close eye on her, of course."

"Absolutely, on both counts. So, when do you leave on your trip?"

"Tomorrow morning. You won't hear from me until I return. I trust you and Ollie will keep the wheels on."

"Certainly. Things will be slow for the next couple of weeks anyway. Hopefully your trip is not all business."

"Morocco is beautiful right now. Be hard not to take a few

hours to myself. And thank you, Dina. I know I'm not always the easiest person to work for. Trust me, I have the utmost respect for you and Ollie. I encourage you both, as always, to speak up when you feel the need."

"I appreciate that. Thank you. If there's nothing else, I have to track down some cake, pizza, and beer for the graduates. Gonna let them cut loose tonight."

Madame shakes her head playfully. They wave to each other. Dina leaves. Madame K gets on her cell phone.

# 31

The three of us, the new Kill Team, walk down the hallway to the elevator on the morning after a fun evening of gorging on cake and pizza, and probably drinking too many IPAs. Vick and I could handle the beer just fine despite the fact we had more than we should have, but Emily, oh boy. Once the suds starting flowing, that girl got silly really quick. We cut her off at just two after asking her if she felt okay and her answer was, "I'm just a little durzy."

It was nice to let loose, hang out, exchange stories, and just smile and laugh. Considering the nature of our work, those moments will be hard to come by. We weren't exactly strangers in this place before last night but the non-job related bonding time went a long way.

Today, we get a sneak peek of our new digs, then we get to go home for a month. For the first time, we finally have the freedom to exit the building through the parking garage without blindfolds and earplugs, and more importantly, without a chaperone, if you don't count the driver. A car is waiting to take us for a preview of the remote team mission house. I've been looking forward to getting some real freedom after a tough few months of training, despite the fact it will be short-lived. I will say, if I had to pick my team, the people I'd have to live with for the next year, I would have chosen Vick and Emily, so I can't complain too much.

As we approach the elevator, Ollie emerges from behind

the sliding doors, heading straight for us. He stops and shakes the hand of Emily and Vick, congratulating them on a job well done and wishing them the best of luck for the future. When he gets to me, he grabs my hands, somewhat aggressively, slipping a piece of paper into my palm as he shakes it.

"Good luck, Josey," Ollie says, locking intense eyes with me. He leans in and whispers in my ear, making sure no one else can possibly hear. "Allister Cole." He lets go of my hand and walks past me.

I'm confused. There's something vaguely familiar about the name but nothing clear comes to mind.

I open the piece of paper and read the words: Want to know who you really are?

I turn to Ollie. "Hey."

He stops and turns just his head back to me before putting his left index finger to his lips. He holds it there for three seconds, then turns and disappears around the next corner.

"You coming?" Emily asks with her head poking out from the elevator, her hand blocking it from closing.

I can't seem to move my feet. "Damn it," I say under my breath, "I can't believe he just did that to me." I will my feet to obey my commands, joining Emily and Vick.

"Everything okay?" Vick asks.

"No. Everything is definitely not okay."

# ABOUT THE AUTHOR

Richard is the author of *Kill Academy* (2017), the exciting new action/suspense/thriller and the first book in a planned trilogy. His previous works include *RejectGuy99* (2015), *A Room Full of Keys* (2013), and *Neither Snow, Nor Rain, Nor Zombie Infection* (2012).

He currently lives in Central Illinois with his wife Amy and Cavachon Padraig. When he's not reading and writing, he spends his time playing disc golf and pickleball, doing DIY projects, playing videogames, watching movies, and hosting amazing cookouts and parties.

www.richardapowellii.com

RICHARD A. POWELL II